On the Wings of Instant Death

Thornton smashed the gunman's face and threw himself out of his car. As he left his seat, he grabbed a short black tube from its mount at the door's base.

The gunman struggled out of the car. Thornton aimed the tube and depressed the trigger mechanism which held a spring-loaded blade in place.

The dagger entered the gunman's chest, ramming through his heart.

SPRINGBLADE
By Greg Walker

SPRINGBLADE

GREG WALKER

CHARTER BOOKS, NEW YORK

To my wife,
Carol,
and our four sons

SPRINGBLADE

A Charter Book/published by arrangement with
the author

PRINTING HISTORY
Charter edition/October 1989

ISBN: 1-55773-266-3

Charter Books are published by The Berkley Publishing Group,
200 Madison Avenue, New York, N.Y. 10016
The name "Charter" and the "C" logo are trademarks belonging
to Charter Communications Inc.

PRINTED IN THE UNITED STATES OF AMERICA

10 9 8 7 6 5 4 3 2 1

ACKNOWLEDGMENTS

I would like to thank J. Butler, L. Maker, T. Halliwell, D. Kelly, S. Davidson, and R. Stewart for sharing their expertise. J. Pollack who knew we could keep it in the SOA family. D. Maurer who took point. Tony Nelson, Hubert Jackson, Chester Golden, who, at one time or another, covered my back and thereby became my brothers. And naturally, my editor, Jim Morris, charter member of the legion whose steps we followed in.

"They made us lose the war after we kicked ass from one end of that place to the other . . . we have a lot more dead friends than live ones. So I have to take my beret from my head, and put it in my heart. I'm not going to put it back on until the enemy has them by the throat. Not until I'm fighting for the Constitution of the United States of America."

Former One-Zero
Special Operations Group

CHAPTER

1

The sapper had slunk toward the camp's wire for over two hours. He had spent the entire day at the edge of the jungle, hidden from view, watching and recording the activities of those who lived behind the walls of concertina and sandbags. He wasn't concerned about barriers. In fact, he was amused at the thought of them. His skill was in penetrating such defenses, and his training had been conducted by a team of North Koreans who were specialists in breaching just the kind of perimeter the Americans thought so effective.

He wore only black shorts and a long-sleeve cotton shirt of the same color. Around his head he had tied the tiger-stripe sweatband he had taken from an American LRRP his platoon had killed in an ambush several months ago. It was one of his prized possessions, like the blue-bladed sheath knife he had recovered from the same ambush. His chest harness was standard NVA-issue pouches filled with only what he needed for his foray this evening. Instead of an AK-47 assault rifle, he carried a captured M-79 grenade launcher, its barrel and stock wrapped in dark cotton to muffle any noise it might make as he crawled over the broken terrain that led to the camp's outer perimeter.

It had taken him four hours to cover the 150 meters between his jungle lair and the site he had selected. Patience was his greatest weapon, something his enemy had meager stockpiles of. This would be his fifth attack against the base in the last two weeks. His mission was simple; infiltrate and disrupt the Americans in the area they considered "safe." He had been successful from the onset, killing the occupants of the obser-

1

vation tower who had unknowingly provided him with an aiming point by lazily smoking their cigarettes as if they were immune to the war.

The tower had been rebuilt, but he noted that it was now so heavily fortified that whoever manned it could not see more than a quarter of what had been possible before his attack. It didn't matter to him what the Americans did with the tower, anyhow. He had drawn a line through its symbol on his target list the very night it fell.

The sapper didn't know that the defenders had nicknamed him "Charlie Brown," after a famous cartoon character back in their country. No one could remember which grunt on the line had coined the moniker, and it wasn't really important. The story that evolved over the mess tables was that Charlie Brown lived just outside the wire and when he got lonely, which was about every other night, he came visiting. When he did, he brought his faithful companion, "Snoopy the Blooper," and Snoopy's bite was far more dangerous than his bark. Despite their levity and wisecracks about him, the bottom line was that Charlie Brown scared the hell out of the grunts. What they couldn't see, they couldn't kill, and they dearly wanted to kill Mr. Brown.

That was a fact that the sapper was aware of, and he took great pains to avoid giving his enemies the opportunity to accomplish their goal. From the security of his spider hole he watched the patrols sent out to destroy him. Several times they had come within meters of where he was hidden. Had it not been for his excellent use of camouflage and the trapdoor's intricate construction of vines and roots, they would have found him. But they hadn't. He would listen to the tone of their voices as they passed within feet of where he sat in his earthen capsule. They were furious at their inability to find him, afraid that he had been watching them throughout their fruitless search, quietly mocking their failure. They were right.

Now he began to settle in and prepare for the night's attack. He would fire three grenades this evening, one more than he usually did. His target was the communications bunker. It was easily identifiable as such from daily comings and goings. The sapper was amused at the formal behavior of the soldiers as they scurried about their business. The salutes and meetings held out in the open by officers with their men had caused him to long for Comrade Trung's very fine Russian sniper rifle. It was certain he could have killed many enemy commanders, a feat that would have resulted in promotion, awards, and perhaps a short leave in Saigon.

It was time. The men in the bunkers normally began to exchange their duties with the new shift of guards at 0100 hours. With new men, freshly wakened, taking their positions from old men, half-asleep, the defenders' ability to quickly pinpoint him once he began firing would be nearly impossible. He had guided himself into position by using his compass along with the constant hum of the gasoline generators which provided power for radios in the bunker. He was not concerned with the strike of the first round, as it was meant only to announce his presence and cause the Americans to "pop" the white parachute flares they so heavily depended upon. Once they lit up the heavens, he would use their own light to accurately fire on the bunker, relying upon his exceptional skill with the launcher to inflict the desired damage.

Atop the rebuilt observation tower, Staff Sergeant Beaumont "Bo" Thornton and Sergeant Wily Carlson lay on their bellies and took turns sweeping the ground beyond the perimeter with their Starlight scopes. The night-vision devices converted the darkness into a world that could be viewed in shades of luminescent green, allowing the men to "see" what others on the line could not. Both scopes were mounted on specially built M-14 rifles, capable of delivering pinpoint accuracy up to one thousand meters.

Requested by the camp commander through the "old boy" network, Thornton and Carlson had been detached from their assignment with Command and Control North (CCN) to help solve the sapper problem. When called in by his team leader and told of the unusual request, Thornton had exploded. "Why in the hell do we have to provide support for a bunch of legs?" he groused. "Can't they kill their own damn dinks? Since when does SOG supply roach-fucking-killers on demand?"

Captain Craig had leaned back in his non-regulation desk chair ("borrowed" from a Marine Corps major in the rear) and fixed his best One-Zero with as serious a look as possible. "We only supply 'roach killers' to those straight-leg colonels who graduated in the same West Point class as the Old Man. Need I say more?" As Craig saw the light come on in Thornton's eyes he rolled forward and pulled several sheets of typewritten paper from a pile casually arranged on the teak-topped desk that had been "borrowed" from a Naval commander at Cam Rahn Bay.

"These are your orders as well as Sergeant Carlson's. Present them to Colonel Elliot when you arrive. Naturally, he's expecting you. The Old Man's given you both to Elliot for five days, period. Solve their problem earlier, and you've got whatever time is left to yourselves. You copy all that, Bo?"

Thornton managed an evil smile as he accepted the paper work with the same display of fervor a man has when asked to pick up a fresh dog turd with his bare hands. "I read you loud and clear, *Dai Uy*. All Wily and I have to do is fly down to this fucked-up firebase, locate some gook with a seventy-nine, nail his nasty hide to the latrine wall, and we get some free time as payback. Is that a good copy, Captain?"

Craig stood and stretched to the full length of his compact five-foot-nine frame. "You got it, Sarge. Draw what you think you two might need from supply, any complaints from our REMF supply sergeant should be referred to me . . . and, oh, I do have just one question for you."

"Sir?"

"Why the fuck are you still here?"

Thornton's face broke into a huge grin. "If you're referring to Vietnam, sir, it's because my orders out haven't been cut yet. But if you mean your office, well, I just wanted to make sure that the omnipotent infantry officer didn't need his floor swept, or his ashtray emptied before the lowly enlisted swine left for the land of non-airborne qualified motherfuckers."

Thornton barely escaped through the open door as Craig's full ashtray hit its frame. As Thornton made his way across the SOG compound, he was followed by Craig's unrestrained laughter. That's a good motherfucker, he thought as he headed for Wily's hooch . . . for an officer.

After Wily and Thornton had drawn their gear, they hitched a ride to the administrative LZ just outside the compound. Elliot had sent his personal chopper to pick the team up, and it wasn't long before the object of Charlie Brown's attentions swam into view below the Huey's skids.

At touchdown, the two SOG operatives were picked up by a hopelessly rotund Sp-4 who served as the colonel's driver and all-around, general-purpose gopher. He pranced about Thornton and Carlson as if they were movie stars, offering to load their equipment into the jeep. His feelings had been obviously hurt when the two soggers refused to allow him even to lift one of the specially built rifle cases off the bird.

Depositing them at the Tactical Operations Center (TOC), where they were to meet with Colonel Elliot, Specialist Blimp scooted off to the motor pool to perform a quick wash job on the jeep. Afterward it would cart his doughboy-like figure down to the ville, where he had plans to soothe his damaged ego with cheap beer and an even cheaper companion. Carlson commented to Thornton as the obnoxious little clerk drove off that perhaps they could find an unattended M-79 lying around and leave it under the specialist's bunk. A few carefully placed explosions around the camp's perimeter that evening, a Hollywood-like foot chase, and lo and behold, the colonel's own driver is the Mad Sapper! "It's got potential, Bo," whispered Carlson as they sat outside Elliot's door.

Before Thornton could comment on Wily's plan, the colonel's voice summoned them into what would be a two-hour briefing on how badly he wanted Charlie Brown's hide nailed to his latrine's wall.

After the briefing, Thornton took everything the colonel had given him and began deciphering the information he and Carlson could use. Wily went about breaking out the rifles, scopes, and other gear they had drawn from the supply sergeant at their own compound. Their primary weapons were the long guns. It was Carlson's job to assemble each one and to then check their operations and functioning. To do so, he sat alone in one of the two rooms provided by Elliot for their use. In the outer office, Thornton finished his analysis of the last two weeks' harassment. There was a definite connection to the location of targets the gook had selected and from where all the reports stated the sound of the grenade launcher had come from. If Thornton's analysis was correct, the team needed only to situate itself so that their rifles covered a specific portion of the base's outer perimeter. When Charlie Brown struck again, they might just get the chance to put the cross hairs on him.

It was time. He had loaded the launcher prior to beginning his crawl through the hell that was the outer perimeter. Dragging the weapon behind him so that both hands were free to search for booby traps and flares. He had felt his way around every device they had placed to either kill him or alert themselves to his presence. His position had been well chosen. A natural depression, it was not more than six inches deep and four feet in length.

Fate decreed that it faced the base, making it possible for him to lie on his belly while observing the camp's normal nocturnal activities. He was close enough to hear men inside the bunkers begin to gather their equipment as they prepared for the changing of the guard. Placing the compass closer to his face, he verified his position to that of the bunker; roughly 150 meters to his front. When the first round impacted, he would assume the standard kneeling position of the grenadier and wait for the flares to illuminate his target. His supply of grenades was secured across his chest in their individual pouches. As soon as one left the tube he would break the gun open, retrieve a round from the harness, loading and firing until all three fragmentation grenades were expanded. Then he would ease back down into his shallow grave to await an opportune moment to safely slither back into the jungle.

"I've got something at my one-o'clock," whispered Wily. He lay several feet from where Thornton kept his own watch, on top of the newly rebuilt tower. Both men had slipped inside during the late afternoon, having their rifles brought up by the regular rotation of guards assigned to the observation post. When darkness settled in, they clambered onto the tower's sandbagged roof through the trapdoor, which allowed access to the tiny platform.

"What am I looking for?" Thornton asked. Hearing the urgency in Carlson's voice, he immediately switched his own scope on and awaited further instructions from his companion.

"Come right to where the water trailer sits," said Carlson. Thornton gently pivoted his weapon so that the trailer slowly emerged inside the optic's viewer. When he was where Carlson wanted him, he grunted an acknowledgment indicating for the sergeant to continue. "Now sweep slowly toward one o'clock. You should pick up a clear area, maybe three or four feet across, about fifty, maybe seventy-five meters outside the wire. Tell me when you're on it."

Thornton gradually moved his rifle as Carlson had dictated. With his forearm resting on a platform made up of two sandbags, the weapon slid easily as if it were held by an imaginary bolt. The bottom sandbag was full, creating a base for the second bag. It had been filled to only three-quarters of its capacity. This had allowed Thornton to fluff the second bag to his liking, every sniper having his own preference in how he prepared his shooting position.

Slowly, so as not to overshoot the clearing Carlson had identified, Bo slid the rifle a millimeter at a time toward the one-o'clock position on their imaginary clock. There it was! The clearing was roughly seventy-five meters from the first strand of concertina wire that encircled the camp. "Got it," he whispered, his voice muffled by the cheek pad he had affixed to the M-14's stock.

Carlson closed his eye for just a moment, then squinted through the Starlight at the clearing he had directed Thornton onto. The scope was an awesome tool in the right hands, but it demanded that a shooter take a break every ten minutes or his eye would begin to experience a condition referred to as "scope-burn." The otherworldly coloration emitted by the scope became tiresome as a marksman focused his attention on a target area for extended periods. Unless he broke away and rested his eyes for a few moments, he could become incapable of making a shot when it was available. For this reason, sniper teams took turns observing, never giving one man too much time behind the scope.

"Right of center, Bo, something . . . something round where there shouldn't be anything round. Can you see it?"

Thornton closed his eye for just a second. Opening it again, he let his mind clear, willing himself to see only what was truly there in the optic's field of vision. He was just about to tell Wily he had identified the round object as a head when the hoarse cough of the seventy-nine announced that Charlie Brown was back in town.

Slipping the safety off, he didn't bother to raise himself any higher than was necessary for the projectile to clear the wire fence. He felt the sharp recoil of the launcher against his side, knowing that the grenade was spinning its way somewhat to the right of the TOC. Its impact pushed a wave of concussive shock across the small parade ground located center-camp. Two deuce-and-a-half drivers were killed as the fury of the exploding grenade unleashed itself just outside the entrance to the mess tent. Both men had been in-country for just three weeks.

Raising himself to his knees, the sapper expertly broke the gun in half and flung the spent shell casing aside. Reaching into his harness, he pulled the first of his three bomblets for the night from its pouch, inserting it deftly into the weapon's breech. In one swift motion, he snapped the receiver closed and positioned the stock so that it was securely snugged into the pocket of his shoulder. Snapping the safety off, he waited for the first flare to burst, wanting only to see the bunker's squat shape beneath its stark glow.

"Got the fuck!" shouted Carlson. "Do you have him, Bo? The bastard is almost standing up!" The explosion and the following confusion negated the need for any form of tactical noise discipline between the two soggers.

Thornton heard the sapper's forty mike-mike shattering the night's calm somewhere to his left rear. There was a wretched little scream followed by healthy, angry shouts of "Medic!" and individual snippets of movement that registered at the very edge of his consciousness while he concentrated on the kneeling figure outside the wire. "Got him, Wily," he said in a slightly higher-than-normal tone. Bo adjusted his left hand so that it encircled the rear sling mount of the weapon, then pulled the stock tightly into his shoulder.

"What's he waiting for?" asked Carlson, who had also zeroed the sapper, and was waiting for Thornton's instruction to fire.

"Flares! The little cocksucker planned to use our own flares to light up his target. We've got a real damned pro out there, Wily. No wonder the colonel's boys couldn't catch his ass." Thornton slipped the safety back through the rifle's trigger guard and began to pull up the slack.

Where were they? Why wasn't the sky lit up with floating candles? The sapper's sixth sense told him that something wasn't right. Never had it taken more than thirty seconds for the flares to begin lurching upward from the camp's defensive positions. And where were the hopelessly wasted machine-gun and rifle fire the Americans were so fond of using whenever they were trifled with? Perhaps he should just fire his one chambered round and be gone, he thought to himself. Something was not as it should be.

"Alternate!" commanded Thornton. Yelling the command so Carlson could hear it, he gently tightened his index finger, letting the sudden recoil of the rifle surprise him. Rapidly regaining his sight picture, he heard Carlson's weapon erupt, and then he was back on target, once again squeezing until his shoulder jerked hard at the stock's insistence.

Theirs was the only firing to be heard. Acting on Thornton's recommendation, Elliot had agreed that any other friendly fire would only confuse the team as they attempted to locate the sapper by both sight and sound. The word had been passed. If the shit started, everyone was to hold their fire unless a red star cluster was popped. If that happened, all hell would break loose as a "mad minute" would permit everything Uncle Sam had to be spewed out against the unseen enemy. The colonel's order had included illumination to prevent "washout" of their scope's illumination.

He was just pulling the trigger when the first round slammed into his left shoulder. The round ripped through the sapper's lean arm muscles, and began tumbling as it blossomed up inside his upper left lung. Exiting, the bullet gutted the man's upper back, leaving a hole the size of a small melon. The shock of the impact knocked the sapper rearward so that he landed on his buttocks. As his mind registered that he was wounded, he used his right hand to reposition the launcher so that the tube rested in the bony, narrow valley formed by his kneecaps as he squeezed them together. One shot, he pleaded with the gods, only one last shot at the enemy!

When the next round struck the firing pin's face plate, causing the weapon to disintegrate in the sapper's hands, his first thought was that the second grenade had exploded inside the tube. But had that been the case, he reminded himself, he wouldn't be feeling the hundreds of burning steel and plastic needles which perforated his arms, chest, neck, and face. Nor would he be awash in the hot, aromatic bath that was his own blood, running like a freshwater stream down the front of his torso. A lucky shot, he thought to himself. I must stand! I must see if I, too, was blessed with a lucky shot!

Thornton's third and final round brought the curtain down. As he watched the sapper raise himself up out of the ground where he was hidden, Thornton locked the scope's cross hair directly center-chest and sent the shot home. Boring through the sapper's now-blood-soaked combat harness, it struck one of the remaining forty-millimeter grenades. The daisy chain reaction that followed lifted the sapper's body high into the air and tore it into thousands of pieces of bone, muscle, and connecting fiber. Charlie Brown left his war-torn world in a thunderclap of vaporous mist, his final score left open in the black notebook still safely tucked away on the earthen shelf of his now-forever-vacant hole.

Colonel Elliot himself drove the two men to their waiting chopper the next morning. As he helped them load their rucks and rifles onto the Huey, Carlson asked where the colonel's driver was. "The dumb bastard hooked up with some bitch who slit his throat from one ear to the other," yelled Elliot over the scream of the chopper's turbine. "The MPs found his ass draped over the hood of my jeep downtown early this morning. A real mess he made of it. Probably have to be repainted before I can use it again."

Wily shot a quick glance to Thornton, who merely shrugged as he shook the colonel's hand. "Appreciate the ride, sir. We'll contact Captain Craig after we've landed." Elliot nodded his understanding as he backed away from the bird, its skids already leaving the hard-baked LZ of red clay before the officer was clear of the rotor wash.

After a twenty-minute flight, they landed at Tri Ton, where they caught an Air America transport to Bangkok. That evening Captain Craig was amused to hear his One-Zero's rather sanitized report of the event via long distance. It ended with Thornton reminding Craig of the captain's promise of unrecorded time off if they completed the mission early. "I know what I said, Bo, but fucking Thailand? How the hell do I explain to the Old Man that you and your sidekick are staying at the Opera House in downtown motherfucking Bangkok? You and I both know that wasn't what his thoughts were when he loaned you out to Elliot."

The line snapped and popped for several moments. Then Thornton's voice reappeared as if he were using the phone in the next office. "Tell the Old Man that his West Point butt buddy was so pleased with us that he insisted we come. Hell, we'll be back in three days, *Dai Uy*, even bring ya something you won't need a shot for afterward."

Craig heard the line go dead. As he hung up the receiver he shook his head slowly from side to side. The walk from the CP back to his hooch near the beach relaxed him. Two teams were going over the wire tomorrow. His wouldn't launch until next week. The Old Man wanted them to place some beacons up on the border between China and North Vietnam. "Fuck it, Bo," he muttered to himself before entering the single-room cabin that was his home. "Sleep well in Bangkok, because for sure we won't be sleeping next week."

He laughed as the surf threw spray against his porch.

CHAPTER

2

It had not been the sounds of guns crashing that had awakened Thornton from his sleep, but rather the steady, ever-present drumming of surf against the shoreline. As he lay alone in the comfort of his beach-side room, he wondered what it was that had triggered his subconscious into pulling up the memory of that night in Vietnam with the powerful intensity that only a dream can have.

Rolling onto his side so that he could look through the partially drawn curtain, he added a conscious postscript to his encounter with the VC sapper and Colonel Elliot. He and Carlson had spent the remainder of the week holed up in the hotel reserved for those Special Forces personnel who appreciated the courtesies offered by the Opera House. Upon their return to CCN, they had launched into North Vietnam along with the rest of the team, only to find that the mission had been compromised by an intelligence leak at MACV. On the ground waiting for them had been a full company of specially trained NVA regulars whose job it was to find, fix, and annihilate SOG teams such as theirs.

Chased for nearly a klick, the team was finally able to gain the top of a small hill where they set up a tight perimeter from which to fight. Craig had been forced to call in minigun fire from Cobra gunships on station, sometimes so close to their own position that the only protection available was the corpses of enemy soldiers who had fallen directly in front of the team's muzzles. By tugging the torn and sometimes still-breathing NVA on top of themselves, the soggers were able to ignore the "danger close" restrictions regarding cannon and machine-gun fire as stated in the regs. Skittering and hovering above the hilltop, gunship crews gritted their teeth and cursed into their intercoms as they attempted to surgically stitch bursts of tracer fire into surges of enemy figures struggling to gain the high ground.

Below, Craig poured on encouragement through the radio link between the fliers and the team. He stopped only to bury his face into the ground as errant minigun rounds hunted and pecked their way into the perimeter, sometimes chewing at the body of a North Vietnamese regular who had been provided by Thornton as a fleshy barrier for his officer's safety. Two Hueys were finally able to get in, the first dropping off a Spike team which threw up an impassable hurdle of steel ball and flechette, over which the assaulting Vietnamese could not climb.

Wily was killed during the team's final dash for the safety of their extraction ship, his body barely recovered when the Cobras came back in to pound the NVA as the Spike team departed. When they got back to the launch site, it was found that everyone on the team had sustained at least one major wound.

It was Thornton's third tour, his last, and the meanest of the three.

Sitting up, he decided to begin this, the third day of his vacation, with a run on the beach. Pulling on a pair of light blue nylon running trunks, he quickly shrugged into a gray sweat shirt with the sleeves cut off at the shoulders. He fitted a year-old pair of Etonic running shoes over his sockless feet, noting that it was nearly time to invest in a new pair, given the shoes' soiled and worn condition. Taking care to plug the Farberware coffeepot in as he passed through the kitchen alcove, he reminded himself that it was the little things such as coffee that the Breacon Point Hotel provided which had caused him to return whenever he had the opportunity.

He had driven into Cannon Beach several years earlier while on leave. After visiting a friend from the Forces who had settled in Portland, Thornton had borrowed the man's '63 Corvette and driven out to the coast. The town reminded Thornton of what Carmel by the Sea must have been like before it had succumbed to the influx of tourists who had discovered its simple charm and good manners.

He had planned to stop only long enough to gas the car and order a quick bite to eat. As it turned out, though, he spent the rest of his leave at Breacon Point, returning to Fort Bragg with a determination to live on the coast. Since that first visit, he returned whenever his duties allowed, this current stay being his first since he and the sergeant major had opened Heavy Hook.

Thick sand tugged at his feet as he trudged down toward the darker hardpack, where the ocean had hammered it into submission. It was early yet, with only a few solitary figures roaming the beach or out jogging. Coming to a stop where the waves' foamy topping collected on the shoreline, he spent several moments staring out to sea. Turning over fragments of the dream, he wished Wily Carlson a warrior's farewell. Thornton seldom reflected on Vietnam, and then without guilt. He had taken the war in stride, regretting only the loss of his friends, the waste of his men, and the senseless victory of his enemy.

His exercise regimen was a simple one. Extending himself to his full height of six three, he began stretching each portion of his body in the slow, methodical way he had been taught in scuba school at Key West. As his muscles and joints began to loosen up, he deepened his breathing, pulling in the freshness of the ocean's air, replacing the stale atmosphere that had built up inside him during the night. After fifteen minutes of careful preparation, he was ready to run.

His first morning on the beach, he had elected to jog a three-mile route. Running south, away from the downtown area, he ran toward a cluster of small homes that had been built on the bluffs overlooking the water. Roughly a mile from Breacon Point, he began to concentrate on establishing the kind of steady pace known among paratroops as the "Airborne Shuffle." Not too fast, yet certainly not a snail's pace, the Shuffle allowed a trooper to run great distances without tiring. It was an endurance builder, a morale strengthener, a ball buster when necessary, and the only way Thornton knew how to run.

Once he reached his turnaround point he picked up the

pace so that by the time he crashed through his imaginary finish line back at the point, he was averaging a seven-minute mile. After a cooling-down period, there followed one hundred push-ups, an equal number of sit-ups, and another fifteen minutes of stretching.

On the eve of turning forty, Bo Thornton had the endurance and flexibility of a man ten years his junior. He never tipped the scales at over 200 pounds, preferring to stay between 190 and 195. His years of exposure to physical conditioning and the martial arts had influenced him toward a lean, graceful physique. He had only recently begun wearing his hair longer than the military had required, and women seemed to find the depth of his oak-colored eyes intensely appealing. He had never married, aware that no woman could have understood his love for the organization he belonged to, or would have wanted to share it with him.

At just that moment a petite young desk clerk was politely informing a caller that Mr. Thornton didn't appear to be concerned with answering his phone. She would gladly take any message he might like to leave, and, jotting down the caller's name and number, she activated the message light connected to room 307's phone.

Privately she hoped he would decide to visit. On a strictly non-professional basis she found him attractive, and the possibility of being seduced by a guest held a particular fascination for her.

Command Sergeant Major (ret.) Frank Hartung dropped the phone's receiver back onto its cradle and resumed drinking his third cup of coffee for the morning. He knew Thornton's habits well enough that he wasn't surprised by Bo's not answering the phone. "Probably out running his ass off again," he mused, glancing through the morning's paper. Spilling some coffee across the headlines, Hartung decided that the news wasn't particularly newsworthy, and forgot about the paper. It was the same old shit anyhow. Nothing really ever changed, just the names and faces of who was doing what to whom. Hartung had spent thirty years either doing it or having it done to him, and he wasn't much surprised at anything anymore.

Coming around from behind the display counter, he prepared to open the shop for business. It was going to be another hot day in San Diego; already the thermometer had hit seventy, and it wasn't even 0800 yet! The dive shop was Bo's notion, and he had asked Frank to help him run it just before the sergeant major retired. Both men were well grounded in scuba operations, having taken their training at the Special Warfare Center's school in Florida. Hartung had been team sergeant for a scuba detachment in the 5th Group at one point, and Thornton had helped develop the Combined Services dive course on Okinawa during the war. It had been a natural avenue for them on retirement.

Hartung opened the Heavy Hook Dive Shop six months before its principal stockholder hung up his beret for the last time. The decision to settle in San Diego had been a logical one. The city was a home port for the Navy, and a thriving business center for those who refused to live in the hell that was Los Angeles. With near-perfect weather year-round, diving was a popular recreation form, and Heavy Hook made money its first month open. Another plus was the existence of a Special Forces community centered around the Navy's elite SEALs stationed in San Diego. Along with the "frogs" there was the school for aspiring naval commandos on Coronado Island. Coronado also played host to a multitude of Special Operations units that required advanced instruction in the kind of warfare practiced by the Navy.

At any time, day or night, one could find operatives from the SEALs, Force Recon, the Air Force's Combat Control Teams, DELTA, or the Green berets hanging out at Heavy Hook. Also welcome were selected members of the retired crowd who lived and worked in the San Diego area. Hartung often commented that they knew more about what was currently going on in the world of black warfare than many of the active-duty practitioners.

Thornton had converted the shop's loft so that friends and visitors could meet and relax in privacy. Unofficially tagged "The Locker," it was an R-and-R center that catered to the nation's most professional warrior clans. Its walls were covered with plaques, patches, pictures, and trophies brought back from missions both overt and denied. There were several stout, wooden tables on which to eat or play cards, and a variety of captain's chairs and barstools to sit on. The bar had been built courtesy of the Navy, although it was doubtful that anyone other than the SEALs involved knew that.

There were fold-down bunks set into the far wall for those who needed a place to spend the night, and a complete home entertainment system for those who only wanted some time and space to themselves. The only rules were the sergeant major's, and he implied that he would enforce them with an ornately engraved baseball bat brought back for him from Burma by a Recon Marine. Hartung kept it mounted behind the bar, within arm's reach. It had yet to leave its perch, but there was never any doubt in the visiting commandos' minds that the veteran of two wars wouldn't hesitate to levy the bat upside the man's head who stepped out of line.

As Hartung fussed with the front door's locks, he heard several of the occupants upstairs beginning to stir. An A-team from the 1st Group out of Lewis had flown in for scout swimmer school, and they had quickly made Heavy Hook their home away from training. Frank welcomed the company. He missed the daily comradeship of the professional soldier's circle.

He'd wait for Bo to return his call. In the meantime he needed to check the pool out back and make sure it was properly balanced for the afternoon's dive class. He had also promised to get a line on some of the new Seiko automatics the youngsters from the 1st were hot about. They still needed him, he thought to himself as he peered at the chlorination reading poolside. Just like that hard-ass partner of his who, God bless him, didn't possess the business sense of a goat. MacArthur had been wrong. Old soldiers didn't have to fade away, they could become respectable businessmen if they used their heads and years of skills to their advantage. He chortled out loud at that one. Hartung had fought as a young private under the general in Korea, and firmly believed that no greater officer had served the country than "Dugout Doug."

The pool would pass muster . . . although *someone* had left an empty beer can on its bottom . . . which meant that someone was going to have to go for an early-morning swim in about thirty damned seconds. As Frank plowed up the stairs toward the loft, he couldn't help but wonder why an agent from the DEA wanted to talk to Bo so urgently. Maybe those assholes couldn't get their own watches, either. . . .

CHAPTER

3

Thornton returned to his condominium, intending to jump into the shower before meandering downtown for breakfast. His plans for the day included gift shopping, a trip to a bookstore that specialized in hard-to-find first editions, and a late movie.

Entering the living room he noted the phone's amber flicker. Pulling his sweat-soaked shirt over his head, he dropped it on the thick carpet. Feeling no sense of urgency to check for messages, he decided on a cup of coffee, pouring a steamy mug's worth from the pot. Only after removing his tennis shoes and briskly toweling himself did he return to the instrument.

He was amused, although not surprised, that it was the sergeant major who had called. The girl at the front desk pronounced Frank's name so that it sounded like "Hard-tongue," an understandable mistake. Thornton didn't bother correcting her, and noticed that she seemed quite friendly. Her voice had a provocative rhythm to it, and he resolved that if she was the same gal he'd checked in with, it might be worth dropping by the front desk for a morning paper.

He punched Heavy Hook's number into the phone and sipped his coffee. "Heavy Hook Dive Shop, Frank speaking. How can I help you?"

Thornton grinned at the salesmanlike smoothness in the old soldier's voice. He knew Frank could blister a recruit's skin with drill instructor's abuse, and God help you if you ever screwed up the SGM's duty roster! Tuning up his own voice several octaves, Thornton decided to fuck with his friend for

19

just a few moments. "Yes, you can, my *dear* sir," he trilled. "Do you offer courses in muff diving?"

There was only the slightest hesitation while Hartung formulated his response. "Muff diving? You bet we offer muff diving, pal. Unfortunately my primary instructor is currently out of state, fucking off. But if you'll leave your name and number, I'm sure he'll be more than happy to get back to you. The only question I have is whether you want to be the muff-*er* or the muff-*ee*."

Thornton chuckled into the mouthpiece. "Hey, you old goat, is that any way to talk to a potential customer?"

"Kiss my ass, Thornton. If you want to play games you should disguise your voice. I recognized it as soon as you lisped the first word."

"Lisped!" challenged Thornton. "I've been on vacation less than seventy-two hours, and you're calling me like some mother whose son is off at camp for the first time. What's the matter . . . you miss me or something?"

"Miss you! I miss you like I miss the clap! We've never run smoother or made more money since you dragged your nasty ass out of here and headed north," Hartung responded. "The only reason—and I say again—the *only* reason I called was because some stud from the DEA wants to get in touch with you ASAP."

The term "stud" was short for student. Hartung's use of it betrayed his several stints of duty as an instructor for the toughest course the Army offered. Thornton had gone through Ranger school as a young Spec-4, and he still grimaced whenever he heard the expression used by the hard-bitten cadre to describe the soldiers who were their wards for fifty-eight demanding days. They had kicked his ass, teaching him just what he needed to know, giving him a chance to survive the carnage that would be Vietnam.

"DEA? As in 'drug spooks'?" said Thornton, now serious.

"Yeah. You know an agent by the name of Bailey? He said you two had worked some shit down South a few years ago."

The name clicked. Calvin Bailey had been a SEAL working out of the naval base in La Union, El Salvador. In 1984 the covert war in that country was in full swing. Special Forces had been assigned to conduct the bulk of the training necessary to whip the country's frontier military into a respectable counter-guerrilla force. The SEALs, on the other hand, were tasked with stemming the seaborne flow of arms from Nicaragua into the hands of the insurgents.

To accomplish their mission, they sired indigenous clones of their own organization. Choosing to ignore the ludicrous restrictions that hobbled their participation in combat operations, the SEALs had taken their Salvadoran and Honduran volunteers and forged them into a deadly band of waterborne raiders. Then, together they had taken the war into the enemy's heartland, confirming the arms link while disrupting the guerrilla's ability to cross the narrow gulf at his leisure.

"Yeah, Bailey registers. I met him in the gulf in the middle of '84. Good troop. Worked hard and cared about his people."

Hartung grunted in response. "Why do you think he's calling? Didn't leave a message for you. Just a paper number in D.C. He said you could reach him any time of the day or night."

In the background Thornton could hear the sounds of the shop, now open for business. "How's work?" he asked.

"Easy money," replied Frank. "Looks like everyone who signed up will show for today's class. I checked the pool and all the gear this morning. We're ready to go."

"Anybody we know in on current DEA activity?"

There was a pause while Hartung swiveled around so that he now faced the wall. "Nothing I've heard around here. But I can make some calls. . . ."

Thornton stood and walked over to the sliding glass door. Outside, the sun was lulling the late-risers from their comfortable nests, and the gulls challenged each other to contests of flights that the best of pilots couldn't hope to emulate. He loved it here. If the shop continued to make money he just might be able to swing a house somewhere along the bluffs. Frank could run the business without him. The old nail eater didn't have any intention of leaving San Diego, anyway, and he knew Thornton's desire to live on Oregon's semi-inhabited coast.

"No. Let's wait and see what Calvin wants first. Maybe he's just touching base to say hello. Or perhaps the DEA needs some divers trained and wants a good cover for them. I'll ring him up and let you know."

"You get laid yet?" Hartung asked slyly.

Thornton laughed at the man's unabashed interest in his sex life. He knew Frank was seeing one of their former students, a middle-aged divorcee who had taken up diving as part of her "life after marriage" program. Given Frank's experience after thirty years of whoring around the world, he didn't doubt she found the sergeant major a never-ending well of wickedness. "Not yet, you old bastard. There's hope, though. I think the little gal you talked to this morning might have an itch."

Hartung chuckled. "She sounds like she's young enough to be your daughter, Sarge. That is, if you had a daughter. I would have thought you'd be looking for someone with more maturity."

"I'm old, Frank, but I'm not dead," retorted Thornton. "Besides, maybe she prefers experience to youth."

Hartung struck as if from ambush. "I doubt that! She probably just feels sorry for you, seeing as we both know you lack that quality when it comes right down to it." Waiting for his friend to continue their never-ending bantering, he waved away a customer who held a fifty-dollar pair of fins in his beefy hand. The man rolled his eyes and waited, wondering why he hadn't taken up golf.

"Just give me Calvin's number, Frank. When I want any shit out of you, I'll squeeze your head!"

Hartung rattled off the agent's number. Then the two men discussed upcoming business. Each had explicit faith in the other's ability when it came to Heavy Hook. Hartung's strength was his innate ability to plan. Thornton's lay with his talent at putting those plans into action. Together they had been an awesome team in uniform. In business they were already known as formidable competitors.

With business out of the way, they signed off. Thornton promised to call if anything of interest came out of the contact with Bailey, although he felt it was probably just a social call.

He showered. Afterward, dressed in a black OP shirt, a pair of stone-washed Levi's, and wearing white deck shoes, he prepared to get on with his vacation. Around his left wrist was the ever-present Rolex. On his right hand he wore an eighteen-karat gold ring which bore the SOG death's head and letters CCN. Against his chest, hanging from a gold chain, lay the carved ivory Buddha that had been given him when he first reported to the highly classified unit. "It's been with me through two tours, Bo. Maybe it'll bring you the same luck it did me," Johannson had told him before rotating back to Fort Bragg. Thornton had worn it ever since. The damn thing's seen more action than any four men put together, he thought, massaging the Buddha's tiny figure. Thornton didn't actually believe in the charm, but then, he didn't advocate pissing off things he didn't understand, either. Now the tiny statue was so much a part of him that he hardly noticed it around his neck.

Deciding to call Bailey sometime later in the evening, Thornton secured the balcony door and latched the windows before leaving. One could never tell these days; it was always better to take a few simple precautions than to be found wanting when the shit hit the fan.

Downstairs, he crossed the outdoor parking lot and slipped into the stairwell that led to an underground garage reserved for guests. Parked in the corner nearest the exit ramp was his pride and joy. The black '78 Corvette had virtually every option available. He had purchased it from a woman who, after she bought it, felt the car was "uncomfortable." She had parked it in her garage to resume driving her deceased husband's Ford.

Thornton had seen the ad in the paper, and not believing the price, had called immediately. He was sure that someone else would have already beaten him to the deal of a lifetime. They hadn't. A quick trip across town and a cashier's check for $9,700 had put him behind the wheel. The car was a killer, and he loved it to death.

Walking around the vehicle, he inspected it for tampering. Content that it hadn't been singled out for special attention during the night, he headed for the resort's lobby, hoping that he wasn't reading too much into the brief conversation with the receptionist earlier that morning.

Her pulse quickened a few extra beats when she saw him enter the foyer. He's well put together, she thought as she busied herself with a stack of credit card charges. Much more so than

I remember when he checked in. His eyes seemed to drift around the wood-paneled room, which had been decorated in the style expected by those who visited the ocean rather than living by it. As they touched hers, she experienced a slight flush rising along the back of her neck. He was really quite attractive, she thought, for an older man.

He moved gracefully toward her counter, giving an elderly couple a pleasant greeting just before reaching her. "Would you happen to have this morning's paper?" he asked in a low, nicely modulated voice.

She presented him with her brightest smile, showing off evenly spaced teeth that, at her mother's insistence, had cost her daddy several thousand dollars. "I believe there's one left, sir. Would you like it now, or should I have it sent to your room?"

"The room would be fine," replied Thornton. He placed his key between them, and she was able to confirm that this was the guest in 307. "I'm going out for the day, and I'd rather not have to carry this around with me. Okay to leave it with you until I get back?"

The girl was truly a beauty. She had pulled her long, thick auburn hair back in order to accent high cheekbones and a perfect nose. Her eyes were large, cast in a unique tint of green. The chin was strong, although there was a slight scar just underneath it, perhaps the result of an accident? She was medium height, and unless she made a point of buying her clothes two sizes too small, she was definitely well endowed. Over her apparently self-supported right breast she wore an embossed rectangular plate that read, Welcome to Breacon Point, My Name Is Linda.

He was staring at her. Not staring, really, perhaps reviewing. She liked the way he wore his hair, the dark brown fullness flecked just slightly with bits of gray. She estimated him to be in his early forties, although his trim figure and obvious musculature could have been that of a man much younger. He wore no wedding ring. More important, there was no band of white flesh that would have betrayed his removing one if a wife were somewhere in tow. She'd seen that before, although she had never fallen for the deception. His was a strong face, nothing particularly exceptional about it except for the oak-colored eyes. They were terribly open, not physically, but soul-wise. This was a man who held back no secrets, who carried no shame. He intrigued her.

"Could you suggest a place to eat?" he asked. Slightly startled, she shook herself back to reality, managing an engaging smile that she hoped would cover what she thought he might have perceived as poor manners on her part.

"Have you tried The Cellar on Surf Tide yet? It's got great seafood, and a super prime rib "

Thornton looked above her head at the mariner's clock hung on a narrow spike driven into the wall. "It sounds great," he replied. "Would you like to have dinner there with me tonight?" His eyes caught hers in frank invitation, their intensity somewhat softened as his charm caused them to crinkle at the corners.

Resort policy stated that employees did not, under any circumstance, date the guests. She made that fact quite clear before excusing herself to take an incoming call. Finished, she stared up at him, waiting to see if he'd drop the matter or press on. Inwardly she hoped he wouldn't be impressed by policy.

Thornton was about to go retrograde. Silly of me, he thought. The girl can't be more than twenty-five, nearly half my age. Hartung was right. She could be my daughter, for God's sake. He began to apologize for his trespass when the phone distracted her. Probably a boyfriend, he thought. No ring, although that didn't mean much these days. She hung up and once again looked at him, her hands on the counter, a look of expectancy on her lightly tanned face.

"If I were to check out, do you suppose we could go ahead with dinner?" He stood outside of himself, shocked at his brashness, fully expecting a cold front to descend.

She laughed. It was an exquisite laugh, a healthy laugh. A laugh that brought a relieved grin to his face as it broke over him like a wave striking a coral reef. "You don't need to do that, Mr. Thornton," she said. "I firmly believe that policies are meant as guidelines, and guidelines are not laws. I'd be happy to meet you, say about seven o'clock?"

"I'll be there," he responded. Turning to leave, he couldn't help but think that he hadn't done too badly. Maybe there was hope for him yet?

The food was everything she had claimed it to be. He enjoyed the prime rib, she a seafood gumbo. Afterward they cruised through town, the Corvette's roof panels off, allowing the evening breeze to channel through the car. She wanted to listen to music, and culled through his collection of cassettes, choosing an old James Gang tape. He was surprised at her selection. She glanced over at him when "The Bomber" began to beat its way through the Vette's Bose speakers.

Later in the evening they walked along the same beach Thornton had run. He learned that she was a student at Portland State, and that she was majoring in journalism. She had only one year left before graduation. Deciding to take a year off from school, she'd answered an ad in the paper and ended up in Cannon Beach. She liked just about everything about her job, except the occasional guest who mistook service for servitude. She was not into astrology, although she then told him that she was a Libra. There was no special man in her life. A broken engagement had convinced her that marriage was something to be carefully considered. "A man (or woman) in passion rides a mad horse," she had offered. There were times that she was lonely.

He found her enchanting. She hadn't protested when he took her hand in his, and there seemed an intimacy between them that didn't depend upon time or obligation for its evolvement.

He told her selected things about his background. She had noticed his ring at dinner, and had stroked its careworn surface as he explained its significance to her. Expecting the standard array of questions about Vietnam, he had been surprised when her only comment was on how extraordinary the band's craftsmanship was.

Later, as he opened the passenger door for her, she asked him if he had killed anyone in the war. Watching the glow of a harvest moon playing off her features, he nodded. He asked her if it made a difference, expecting that it would. Again she surprised him.

"You were a soldier in a war," she said. "If your job was to fight, to stay alive, to survive, and come home, then you had to do whatever it took. If killing was required, then that's why you're here tonight. The only difference it would make would be if you hadn't done your job. Because then, we couldn't have met." She was silent after that, staring around him at the rocks where the sea crashed against them in timeless regularity.

"How did you get to be so wise?" he asked.

She looked into his eyes, sadly. "My brother was a Ranger. When they were sent to Grenada, he was killed during the attack on Calvigny." She paused, then continued. "He used to write me letters about being a soldier. Donald was going to be a . . . 'lifer' I think was an expression he used." She moved close to Thornton, stepped around the car's open door, and pressed her face against his chest. His arms encircled her instinctively, as a father would a hurt child. She responded, her hands pressed against his shoulders, hugging him into her, holding him.

"I'm sorry he died," was all Thornton could murmur.

She squeezed him hard in response. "If killing made a difference between us, it would have to with him also. You came back. Don didn't. I can be happy for your being here, can't I?" Her question tugged at him, opening wounds that he had thought scarred over. Curiously, there was no pain in him, only sorrow for her loss. How many letters had he written to the wives and parents of men like Donald?

They drove to her place in silence. Once there, they talked until well past midnight, she falling asleep as they sat on the couch, listening to quiet jazz. Careful not to wake the sleeping girl, he gently carried her to the bedroom, then covered her with a patchwork quilt he found folded on a chair. Locking the door after himself, he strolled out to the 'Vette' and decided on a short drive before heading back to his condo.

The highway was deserted. As he pushed the powerful automobile through its narrow curves, he couldn't help but smile. There wasn't anything like a full-blown Corvette to run down the road in, especially feeling the way he did. It wasn't long before he found himself on a long, straight stretch of coastal highway, the ocean to his left, and tall Oregon pine on the right. Careful of his speed, he kept the car at a conservative sixty miles per, settled back in the custom comfort of his seat.

Thornton saw the glimmer of something shiny long before he was able to distinguish the hitchhiker standing alongside the dark pavement. Dressed in a silver racing jacket and dark pants, the man leaned out and gave the universal hand signal of a man needing a ride. At his feet was a small tote bag, one of those from airport gift shops. Slowing just a bit, Thornton glanced at the stranger as the Corvette shot by. He looks pretty straight, Thornton thought to himself. Probably ran out of gas somewhere or had a flat.

He checked the rearview mirror before pulling off onto the highway's shoulder. Adjusting the mirror so he could see the now-running hitchhiker, he justified this out-of-the-ordinary break in his habits by recalling his own experiences at hitchhiking. Besides, if he didn't like the guy's attitude he could always kick his ass out of the car.

"Hey, thanks for stopping. I thought I'd be out here *forever*." Looking up through the open t-top, Thornton was pleased to see that his passenger was indeed clean-cut, to the point of having a military haircut.

"No sweat. I normally don't give rides, but at this time of the morning it's pretty lonely out here. Hop in. You can throw the bag in the back or slip it on the floor, whatever suits you."

With a nod, the hitchhiker opened the door and slipped into the passenger seat. Setting his pack on the floor between his feet, he gave Thornton another smile and extended his hand. "I'm Jake . . . Jake Bonner."

"Pleased to meet you, Jake, mine's Bo. Where you headed?"

"Just up the road another seven miles or so. I got a place just off the highway."

Thornton powered the car back onto the road, giving the huge engine its head as they easily came up to speed. "So how'd you get stuck out here?" he asked.

The hitchhiker laughed before answering. "My girl friend and I were down on the beach just fooling around, and all of a sudden she gets this big case of the ass at me. Don't ask me why, 'cause I couldn't tell ya. Next thing I know she's in my car, heading down the road. Women. I've never been able to figure them out."

Thornton nodded. Both men sat quiet for the next few miles, each lost in his own thoughts as the Corvette's steady purr lulled them into separate worlds. Finally Thornton spoke. "We ought to be getting near your place pretty soon. What should I look for?"

The hitchhiker turned his body so that his back was snugged up against the car's door. Unzipping the bag at his feet, he reached inside it and removed a nickel-plated .41 Magnum revolver. Leveling the six-inch barrel at Thornton's midsection, he spoke quietly. "You should look for me to blow your fucking guts out if you don't do exactly what I say. Any problems?"

Thornton rolled his eyes upward. Damn, he thought, the one time I play good samaritan and I pick up a whacko. Why me, Lord, why me? Casting a quick eye toward his captor, Thornton shook his head in the negative. "No problems, pal, what's the plan?"

"In a mile or two you'll see a dirt road off to the left. Take it. When I want you to stop I'll say so. You get weird on me, try and play hero or something stupid like that, and you're a dead man."

Several minutes later Thornton recognized the turnout described by the gunman. Seeing no other lights behind or in front of him, he gave up any thought of help. As the low-slung vehicle crunched onto the gravel path, Thornton accepted the fact that his passenger would probably try to kill him. The man was too calm, too sure of himself. Ten to one he'd pulled this scam on other equally unsuspecting motorists whose bodies turned up when some unlucky soul stumbled upon them while out picking flowers.

After a short but bumpy ride, the hitchhiker ordered him to stop. Sitting there, the two men eyed each other, their faces illuminated by the dash's instrument lights, which were still on.

Finally the killer spoke.

"You leave your wallet on the dash, and the keys in the ignition. When I tell you to—and *only* when I tell you—you open up the door and back out of the car. Once you do that I'll let you walk away."

Thornton's mind was racing. "So what you're telling me is that if I play along with you, the only thing I've got to worry about is the long walk back to Cannon Beach, right?"

The man called Jake snorted. "Right. Hey, if your lucky, maybe someone will pick you up. . . ." Thornton didn't join in as the man laughed at his own joke. Seeing he wasn't amusing Thornton, Bonner thumbed the big revolver's hammer back, its click clearly audible in the early morning's quiet.

"The wallet, asshole."

Thornton shrugged. "It's right there on the dash. It's your lucky night, too, pal. There's over a grand in it."

For the briefest second the night rider took his eyes off of Thornton to sweep the dash's surface. As he did so, the pistol's barrel swung away from Thornton, who seeing his ruse had worked, made his move. Deftly jerking the keys from the steering column with his right hand, he smashed them into the gunman's face. Not waiting to see what damage he'd done, Thornton popped his door open, throwing himself out of the car. As he left his seat, he yanked a short black tube from its mount at the door's base, feeling at the same instant the hot rush of a bullet roaring over his hip.

"You *motherfucker*!" screamed Bonner, his face torn and bleeding from where the keys had cut him. "I'm gonna kill you!"

Thornton hit the ground and scrambled back behind the protective bulk of the Corvette's rear deck. Chancing a quick look, he watched the hitchhiker struggle up through the roof's open hatch, his Magnum gripped tightly as the upper half of his body emerged.

Pulling the tube apart, Thornton revealed a long, double-edged blade. Above him, the enraged hitchhiker had finally wiggled his way to a standing position, and scanned the surrounding darkness. Thornton was about to make his move when he heard his name spoken. "Bo? Bo . . . I know you're out there. I'll cut a deal with you if you'll listen." There was a moment's silence before the gunman began speaking again. "Bo, you toss the keys toward the car and I'll just leave you be. No hard feelings, my man. I'll just take the car and let you alone. Whatta ya say?"

Thornton heaved the small stone he'd pried up from the roadway into the darkness. Hearing its impact, Bonner swung his frame so that his back was to Thornton, who was now standing upright. "I say you just fell for the oldest trick in the book . . . asshole!"

Hearing the voice behind him, Bonner attempted to twist the heavy Magnum around for a shot. Thornton, realizing there were no options left, aimed the unusual knife, and depressed the trigger mechanism which held a spring-loaded blade in place.

As soon as he felt the dagger fly free, he threw himself on the ground, rolling into the darkness.

Bonner gasped as the spring-driven steel dart entered his chest via his armpit. As it rammed its way through his wildly beating heart, his knees buckled, and he began to sink down into the Corvette. Thornton waited for the revolver to slip from the dying man's grasp before he approached the vehicle. Cautiously opening the passenger door, he reached inside and pulled the hitchhiker out, careful not to disturb the blade's position in the body. A quick check showed that no blood had splattered the 'Vette's rich interior, although it was now beginning to seep through the satin racing jacket.

Thornton had seen enough men die to know that Bonner had but minutes left. Lifting the tote bag from where it sat, he dropped it next to the man's body. Taking an old rag he carried in the glove box, he retrieved the Magnum and lay it alongside the bag. Squatting down, he waited. It wasn't long before the hitchhiker's breathing stopped, his chest and throat filled with warm arterial blood.

Inching the 'Vette up to the highway, Thornton was relieved to note that it was empty. Pulling the car across the road and parking it, he grabbed a whisk broom he kept under his seat and tied it to the car's tire iron. Retracing his route to the corpse, he began to sweep over the Corvette's tire tracks and his own footprints. A master tracker, Thornton took his time, completing his task just as the faintest glimmer of an approaching car's headlights appeared several miles down the road.

Stowing the makeshift broom behind his seat, Thornton gently eased the sleek racer back onto the highway. Coming up to speed, he ignored the oncoming vehicle when it passed by, satisfied that the driver took no notice of him as its tail-lights evaporated in the distance.

Once back in the apartment, he reminded himself that he was supposed to have called Bailey. A glance at his watch showed it to be well after one o'clock in the morning. Bailey *had* said that the number was good any time of the day or night, and Thornton didn't feel like sleeping just yet. He'd see Linda tomorrow when she returned to work. In the meantime, he wondered how late the DEA let their agents stay up. . . .

Bailey's pager allowed a caller to leave a vocal message, which it then relayed. As Thornton settled his frame into one of the two black leather chairs that sat in his living room, he dialed the number given him by Hartung earlier that day, mentally composing the harassment he felt the agent was due.

At the end of the tone, Thornton spoke quickly into the phone, using his most professional voice. "Good morning, Mr. Bailey. My name is Thornton, I'm your wife's attorney. If this, as well as last month's, child-support payment doesn't arrive by the week's end, I'll be forced to have papers served. Should there be any problems, please contact me at the following number. . . ." Leaving the resort's business number on the recording, Thornton hung up and opened a beer from the fridge.

Five minutes passed before the Breacon's twenty-four hour operator transferred a very embarrassed Calvin Bailey's call to room 307.

"You asshole, Thornton! You can't possibly know how you fucked me over with that little prank of your s." The tone in Bailey's voice reminded Bo of a little boy who had been caught taking money from his mother's purse.

"Easy, Calvin," Thornton replied. "Remember, you're the one who called me . . . and on my vacation yet. Fuck with the bull and you get the horns."

Bailey managed a weak laugh. "Yeah, well . . . let's just say that 'my wife's attorney' just screwed me out of two weeks of charming a particular young lady of whom I am *very* fond. I doubt that she'll ever speak to me again, not to mention consider going out."

Balancing the phone so that he could open the double drapes that covered sliding glass door, Bo made a halfhearted attempt to apologize. "Hey, I had no idea you were romancing this late in the evening, Cal. If it's love, I'm sure she'll see you again, and you can blame the whole misunderstanding on me."

"Love!" exploded Bailey. "It ain't love, Thornton! It's honest-to-God *lust*! This girl's a stone-cold fox, and there ain't no way I'm going to be able to explain this to her. You owe me, Bo."

Thornton brought it back to business. "So what's the scoop, Calvin? You didn't just call for fun and games."

There was a pause at the other end as Bailey realized he had to make this one call count. Get it together, he told himself. You've only got one chance to get Thornton to listen. Fuck it up and you might as well get out the dress whites and re-up. Don't bullshit the old soldier, though, he'll see through you like the man with X-ray eyes.

"No, Bo, I didn't call just to rehash old times. Shit, we only know each other because of those ops in '84. This is business, if you're interested."

"Continue to march, Cal, it's your quarter."

Bailey sighed. He shook a Marlboro from its flip-top box and lit up, using the engraved lighter given him by his team when he left the Navy. Sitting down, he leaned back and gazed out the window. The lights of Washington flickered and blinked in the early-morning hours, and for all their attraction he couldn't help but envy Thornton's being at the beach.

"The people I work for would like to fly you out for a few days. There's a project being put together that we feel you might be interested in. If not, then perhaps you can point some things out about it that maybe we're missing." Bailey blew a steady stream of smoke against the window, watching the mushroom effect as it struck the pane, flaring out toward the corners of the deeply tinted glasswork.

"I'm not coming out for free, Cal. Those days are over. You need a consultant, you pay for one. How deep's the pocket?"

Bailey smiled, seeing his reflection in the nicotine-stained glass and thinking how much he looked like an asshole at that particular moment. "Plenty deep, you mercenary mother-fucker! First-class seating. You'll be put up at The Patriot's Inn, just around the block from my office. All reasonable expenses are on us. If you'll fly, we'll buy."

"Can you clue me in on what we'd be talking about?"

Bailey had foreseen the question and knew he needed to play it right down the middle. No one outside a small circle in the DEA and the White House knew what was being offered as a short-term solution to one of the country's most critical internal problems. "It's a very 'close hold' subject, Bo. Even if I could tell you, I'd have to kill you afterward."

Thornton laughed. "You're on, squid. I'm yours for two days. That's max. Make the arrangements and call me here tomorrow, preferably later in the afternoon. I'll need to fly out of Portland, so allow for a three-hour drive from where I'm staying."

Bailey stubbed his cigarette out. "Any problems getting out tomorrow night?" he asked.

Bo thought briefly of Linda. He'd tell her he had an unex-pected business trip to take, and would she mind watching his car for him? She could drive him to Portland and . . . and maybe she didn't care to see him again after tonight. Perhaps her acceptance had been simply a one-time deal. Why should he think there was anything more to it, or even possible? Aware that Calvin was standing by for his answer, Thornton experienced a strange sensation. Could it be a fear of being rejected? he thought. No. Her embrace on the beach had shown him that if he was careful with her, there was more possible than just one night as friends.

He punched back into the conversation. "Tomorrow night's good, if you can get me out on such short notice."

"That means we can meet on Friday. I've got the morning tied up with a briefing, the same folks interested in what you've got to say. If you can hang loose, we'll meet for lunch and I'll lay it all out. Should everything go okay, you'll be on your way back to the coast Saturday evening."

"Call me tomorrow," Thornton said. He and Bailey shot the shit for a few moments longer, then hung up.

Preparing for bed, Thornton couldn't help but ask himself why he had agreed to meet with Calvin so quickly. Could it be that he missed the adventure that had been a part of his life for so many years? Turning off the light, he shrugged the blanket up around his shoulders and told himself that it was too damn late to start thinking like a college professor. Life was a game of choices, some were good, some were bad. The one thing he was sure of was that he never turned down a free airplane ride, especially if it was first class.

CHAPTER

4

The flight to Washington was enjoyable. Flying first class had its points, especially when you didn't have to pay for it. Linda had been able to beg a day off, although she wasn't excited about his leaving. The prospect of "owning" her own Corvette had helped balance the equation, though, and she looked good behind the wheel. "I'll bring you back something from the capital," he told her before boarding the Delta flight.

"Make it a Washington Redskins T-shirt!" she begged. "They're my favorite team, and you're going to be right there." He promised to look for one, then had to promise that it would be large enough for her to sleep in. "And no jokes about my boobs," she said.

"Lin, believe me, your boobs are nothing to joke about."

She slapped at him playfully just as the loudspeaker announced that first-class passengers, unaccompanied children, and invalids were welcome to board.

He spotted Bailey as soon as he entered the terminal at Dulles. The former SEAL hadn't changed much since '84, although the civilian clothes and longer hair masked his fireplug physique. Strolling over to the DEA agent, Thornton grasped his outstretched hand, shaking it warmly. They both began walking out toward the main terminal, ignoring the crowd.

"You got any other luggage than the carry-on?" asked Calvin.

"Nope. Travel light, travel fast. This is all she wrote," he said, hefting the black cordura suit bag.

"Great! I'm parked just across the street. Let's get the fuck out of here so we can talk."

Stepping into the night, Thornton's senses were immediately assaulted by the difference in weather. Where the coast was cool and breezy, Washington was an uncomfortable stalemate between the day's lingering heat and the evening's coolness. Thornton believed the odds to be in the heat's favor. "You like D.C.?" he asked the quickstepping agent.

Looking both ways as he led them toward the car, Bailey threw an impetuous look at Thornton. "Naw, D.C. sucks, Bo. The humidity is awful, the heat stifling, the people all tuned in to the power game, whether they're a part of it or not. Plus," he added, "it's too close to the flagpole." They reached a low-slung Chevy Camaro with a blood red paint job that must have cost a minor fortune. "This one's ours, pal. You can throw your bag in the trunk. We're going straight to the hotel."

Thornton walked around the back of the car and waited for Bailey to open the boot. There wasn't much room for his bag, but the agent managed to relocate several locked wooden boxes, making it possible for him to shove Thornton's bag into the overstuffed trunk.

"What the hell you packing in there, Cal?"

Snapping the trunk lid shut, the agent snickered. "There's a micro Uzi in the smaller box, plus eight fully loaded additional magazines."

"Naturally," said Thornton.

"The other box has a coupla stun grenades, a gas mask, a cut-down twelve-gauge, and other assorted implements of death and destruction common to all DEA agents who are concerned about the Right to Life issue."

Thornton grunted his approval as he slid into the passenger seat. The balanced and blueprinted 350 snorted to life, and Calvin expertly slid them into the airport's traffic pattern, happily ignoring an oncoming bus as well as an old man trying to gain the safety of the center island. "Life's a bitch in the city," said Thornton, craning his head to see whether or not the old codger made it.

"And then you die," finished Bailey. The drowsy evening

swallowed them up as Calvin threaded the city streets, preferring a route that allowed them time to talk.

By the time they reached the hotel, Thornton knew why
they had brought him to town.

"That's it in a nutshell, Bo," concluded Bailey. "Tomorrow
afternoon we'll attend a briefing with several high-level
staffers from my agency, and they'll fill in the holes. But you
know most of what you'll hear already . . . at least everything I
could tell you."

Parking the Camaro outside the lobby, both men entered.
Bailey checked Thornton in using a credit card. He signed the
bill before they headed upstairs. They were silent during the
elevator ride to the twelfth floor, neither speaking until Thornton had unlocked the door and they were both inside. The
room itself was a cut above standard hotel fare. Decorated in
what the weary traveler might consider "Colonial," it featured
a king-size bed, writing table, two wooden captain's chairs, a
bureau, a phone, and a twenty-one inch color television that
was neatly bolted into the wall.

Bailey turned on the one-eyed idiot and began briskly
snapping through channels. Thornton threw his suit bag on the
bed, unzipped it, and carefully removed his hung items. When
he was finished he pulled up one of the chairs and joined his
friend, who had abandoned television in favor of the view
from Thornton's perch twelve floors above the city.

"I'm going to work up some names, equipment I think
might be appropriate, and some prices before racking out.
Any problem with that?"

Bailey turned away from watching a dope transaction
going down on the corner opposite his observation point. He
crossed the room and sat on the edge of the surprisingly comfortable bed, pulling a short-barreled Smith and Wesson .357
Magnum from under his Windbreaker. "No. I told 'em I'd
brief you tonight so we wouldn't waste time bullshitting
around at the office. Naturally you have to pass muster first,
that's Billings's decision. He's the mission-assessment agent."
Bailey released the weapon's cylinder, spinning it as he
checked all six rounds, then snapping the weapon shut. Looking directly at Thornton, he smiled. "You ready to get some
sleep?"

Thornton nodded. He was tired, although sleep wasn't much of a priority. Long ago he'd learned to regulate his metabolism so that he could go for long periods with minimal rest. He didn't enjoy it, but if it was essential to the mission, he could hang with the best of them. Checking his Rolex, he noted that it was nearing midnight. "What do you want to do in the morning? I can wait here, meet you, or whatever works best."

Bailey reholstered the stout little Magnum. Most of the other agents in his office preferred to carry automatics, counting on high-capacity magazines to give them an edge against the arsenals owned by drug runners. He chose to stick with a wheel gun, comfortable in the knowledge that he was very good with one and liking the power it could deliver.

Several months before, during a pre-dawn raid, he'd had to dump a huge black dealer who called himself "Gypsy." The man had been armed with an AK-47, and had elected to shoot it out rather than take the fall. Hit twice by another agent using a 9mm "Wonder-Nine," the dealer had kept firing at both men until Bailey whacked him with the .357. Later they found the dealer was wearing a lightweight bullet-resistant vest which had been purchased from the same manufacturer who supplied the DEA with their equipment.

"We can do breakfast in the morning," replied Bailey. "I've got to meet some people at nine, but if you're hungry around seven...?"

"That's fine," said Thornton. "Can you drop me off someplace on your way to wherever it is you're going?"

The former SEAL opened his hands, palms outward, shoulders shrugged in the classic Arab gesture that conveyed that all and anything was possible... God willing and the creek don't rise.

"I'd like to visit the Wall," he said.

Bailey nodded. He had wondered if the old warrior would want to do that. Calvin himself had gone; first alone, then later with a group of SEALs taking time off from training at Quantico. Both visits had been humbling. Bailey himself had not served in Vietnam, the war having ended before he even considered joining the Navy. But after his recruitment in college, along with the missions he'd been part of in both Central America and the Middle East, he knew what war, sacrifice, politics, fear, loss, and frustration were all about.

The Wall's gift was an ability to comfort rather than condemn. It was a place of group solitude, with a sense of both physical and spiritual solidarity with the 58,132 combatants who had finally succeeded in striking down the term "ignored." Bailey had been deeply moved by what the Wall could draw from its visitors. It permitted him to drink from his own well of sorrow when he discovered the name of a friend who had joined the Marine Corps after high school in 1968.

Larry had been a typical high-school success story, a gifted athlete, better-than-average student, and a favorite with the girls. Welker was the kind of guy you wanted to have as your friend, because if he was you became somebody special, too. A year after becoming a Marine, Larry was dead. He had been shot in the face by a Vietnamese teenager he had attempted to befriend during the sweep of a suspected enemy village. Bailey hadn't thought about Larry Welker until the day he recognized the photo-stenciled-etched name on one of the 140 panels that made up the Wall. In the skip of a heartbeat he'd been back in the stands at Prospect High watching Larry throw the final pass of the Thanksgiving Day shoot-out with their rival, Saratoga. That pass had clinched the championship for them, a moment frozen in each of their lives when they had all been winners in a world whose rules they understood.

In that moment he missed him terribly. He also wondered whether anyone in Larry's outfit had killed the little bastard who had murdered his schoolmate. It was only then that he started to cry.

Then Bailey was back, shrugging himself like a man awakening from a spell, rolling his shoulders and standing so abruptly that Thornton was startled. Bailey returned to the window, hands thrust deeply into the pockets of his Levi's, his back straight and feet spread as he answered Thornton's question.

"I thought you might," he said. Turning to sit on the narrow sill, Bailey folded his arms across his chest. "The best way to be ready for the Wall is to not be ready for it. You'll understand what I'm saying once you're there. I'll drop you at

Constitution Garden after we eat. It's just a short walk to the memorial."

It was Thornton's turn to nod. He stood and walked over to where the agent sat. Stretching out his hand, he said, "Thanks for the taxi service. I'd better get some shut-eye if I'm going to appear halfway intelligent to your bosses. I'll see you in the lobby about seven o'clock." Bailey grasped Thornton's hand, shaking it firmly. "Damn glad you came out, Bo. Don't mind my somberness; the Wall's a heavy place. It affects everybody who goes there differently. Have a good night's sleep and we'll talk business tomorrow."

As Thornton walked him to the door, Bailey reached under his coat, around to the middle of his back. When his hand reappeared it was holding what Thornton recognized as a BaliSong folding knife. "If all you've got is carry-on, then I doubt you brought an 'equalizer' with you."

Thornton shook his head. It was nearly impossible to bring any kind of adequate weapon on board a commercial airliner since the United States had begun taking terrorism within its own borders seriously.

Bailey handed the knife over to Thornton. "Keep this until you leave on Saturday. D.C. sucks crimewise, and as I recall, you're supposed to be pretty good with a blade." He watched as the former Green Beret mentally judged the weight and balance of the Filipino fighter, then in a whirl of sparkling steel the knife was open and locked, cutting edge up, ready to slash, thrust, and kill if necessary.

"Thanks," said Thornton. "I've always liked deAsis's work. I'll take good care of it for you, although I doubt I'll need it." Slipping the lock, he reversed the opening motion, the knife's blade slapping back between the two aluminum "wings" with a resounding *clink*.

I've never been able to do that, Bailey thought as he stepped into the lift. He shrugged, shaking his head from side to side as the elevator's doors softly sealed him inside the sterile chamber. There were a lot of things that only Bo Thornton could do, and this mission was one of them. The meeting tomorrow between Thornton and the DEA would determine

the course of the country's war on drugs. He hoped Thornton
would listen to what they said. Because they needed him
again . . . except this time in America.

He was just unlocking the Camaro's door when a voice
hissed at him from out of the darkness. "Hey, my man, that's a
nice ride you got."

Turning slightly, Bailey recognized the speaker as one of
the men he'd watched from Thornton's room earlier. Ignoring
the compliment, the narc pulled his keys free from the door
and slid into the driver's seat. As he turned the big engine
over, he rolled his window down, letting in the night's cool
air. Without warning he felt a hard, cold object pressed up
against his temple, the click of the revolver's hammer almost
painful to him.

"Man with a car like this has to have money, too," the oily
voice whispered. "So why don't you just give it up . . .
honky?"

Calvin allowed a burst of air to escape his mouth. Slump-
ing down like a man who knows when he's been licked, the
Fed slowly turned his head so that the gun's barrel now
pointed directly at his forehead. "Be cool, brother . . . be
cool!" he intoned. "I don't want no trouble, man. The wallet's
inside my coat. . . ."

A slit of a grin split the mugger's features. "Get your hands
on the wheel where I can see 'em . . . and the cash better be
there or I'll blow your damn eyes out! You hear me, boy?"

Placing his hands where the gunman had ordered, Calvin
began wishing he wore his badge around his neck rather than
carrying it in his wallet. Knowing the asshole would go
bonkers when he discovered he was robbing a cop, Bailey
began slowly easing his foot off the clutch, the Camaro already in first and the parking brake off. With any luck he'd be
fifteen feet downwind before the doper could pick himself up
off the ground. Then it would be Smith and Wesson time.

Just as he felt the transmission begin to engage, the mugger's hand snatched at his wallet, then released it as another
hand closed over the tiny .38 held against Bailey's head. In an
instant the window was vacant, only the sound of a feeble
struggle coming up from the pavement.

Risking a look, Bailey was startled to see Thornton. The

big man's knee was buried in the mugger's back, effectively pinning the squirming figure against the asphalt like a butterfly on a dissecting board. Glancing up, Thornton handed the man's weapon to Bailey, then pulled the BaliSong from his pocket. In one graceful motion the wicked blade was fully extended and locked into place.

"Move one more time, dicklips, and I'll cut your nuts off!" snarled Thornton. Immediately the streetwise addict ceased his struggle. "Whatta we do with him?" The question was directed to Bailey.

"We could call the cops...." Bailey's unexpected answer caused Thornton to look curiously at the federal agent. "Or we could teach the bastard a lesson ourselves."

Thornton nodded. Leaning down, he whispered into the man's ear, grunts of comprehension his reward as the mugger acknowledged Thornton's suggestions. Pulling the man to his feet, the ex-Beret hop-stepped him across the lot. Before releasing the unfortunate holdup artist, Thornton offered one last piece of advice.

"Fuck with the bull, my man, and you get the horns. I suggest you think about it . . . on your way to the hospital."

With two powerful, pistonlike movements, Thornton slammed the BaliSong deeply into each of the man's fleshy buttocks. As the would-be mugger's body collapsed in shock, Thornton knelt and plunged the dripping blade into the neatly manicured grass on which the babbling street trash lay. Satisfied, he carefully folded the knife back into itself and walked back to Bailey's still-rumbling Camaro.

"What'd you tell the asshole?" asked Bailey, a Marlboro hanging from his lips.

"I explained how it wasn't too smart to try and rob someone in full view of an open window . . . which is where I was at when I saw you step on your dick down here."

Bailey chortled. "Yeah, no doubt about that. Fucker had me dead to rights until you showed up."

Thornton playfully cuffed the younger man on the side of the head. "Don't sweat the small stuff, Cal. I had you covered all the way."

Snubbing his half-smoked cigarette out, Bailey snorted in

disgust. "Fucking dopers, muggers, whores, rip-offs . . . shit, the night's full of 'em."

Thornton turned and headed for his room. Somewhere across the city a siren began its high-pitched yelp, others joining in as the wheels of justice began to roll.

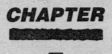
The "Wall" is actually two such structures. Each of its septums measures 246.75 feet in length, and where they meet they form an angle of 125 degrees. At its highest point, it stands a full 10.1 feet, the Wall at both ends commencing at nearly ground level. One hundred forty individual black granite panels form the engraved face. In chronological order they display the names (first, last, middle initial) of the 58,132 men and women who died or are listed as missing in action.

The controversy that surrounded the memorial's birthing is a microcosm of the conflict that seeded it. Some veterans considered the Wall an appropriate tribute to their experience, others viewed the architecture as a "black gash of shame," demeaning the sacrifices made by both the living and the dead. In the end, though, it was built. Then, to appease the detractors, a flagpole flying the nation's flag was erected, a bronze statue of three Vietnam-era infantry soldiers standing mute watch over their brothers in arms was emplaced, the sculptor's skills so incisive, the feeling of the site so right, that often hands stretch forth to touch the figures as if wanting to reassure them that all is well.

In 1986 nearly five million people walked the silent path that leads to the legacy of Vietnam. More than any other war memorial, the Wall reflects the gravity of its visitors' emotions. Through their gentle sobs, caressing fingers, innocent kisses, cherished pictures, searching notes, and surrendered medals, the bonds once broken are mended. The ranks of dead stand erect. Their granite-etched profiles mystically rendered alive through their names; Terry A. Dennison . . . James F.

Askin . . . Matthew Smith . . . Leroy Barnes . . . Charles E. Hawk.

Their names are a tally sheet of the price paid for political folly. The quiet yet forceful message is clear . . . war cannot again be so easily undertaken.

Strangely there is no specter of defeat. Perhaps it is impossible for it to exist in a place that gladly opens its arms to the most contrary of human emotions, love and loss. This is a place where men hold each other without shame, where their tears can flow without restraint, where medal-laden chests heave mightily as they release their long-carried grief. There are no strangers at the Wall. Here desolation is vanquished, solitude is shared. Memories are activated by a touch, a word, a threadbare unit patch carefully sewn to a new field jacket. Defeat? Hardly.

It was to this place that Thornton journeyed; driven by his own need to draw back the curtain, to face himself in the reflection of his comrades' deeply polished memorial. By touching the Wall he could lose touch with the war. He sought peace within himself. If it could be found through an appointment with the dead, then so be it.

He watched Bailey drive off, standing still until the Camaro was out of sight. He then entered the expansive grounds that formed a protective buffer against the city's unfeeling bustle. Even at this early hour there was a crowd on the street. Many were going to work; many more were tourists trying to get as much sight-seeing in as possible. Still, there weren't many visitors as he signed the Wall's official log and strolled down to its base. While signing his name, he noticed that there was a guide for those looking for a specific person. He had quickly glanced over the computerized lists, a sense of unease rising within him as he reviewed the roles of the dead. Thornton had served three tours in Vietnam. There were a lot of names that he would know. How many would he find that he hadn't known were there?

He spent the entire morning at the memorial. It was awesome in its impact. Beyond explanation, far too private an experience to attempt to share with anyone, except for perhaps someone who had been there. He lost count of the times he walked the memorial from end to end. When he had to pull away he withdrew to the statue, captivated not only by its uncanny representation of men he once knew, but how much of himself he saw in their eyes.

And the eyes! They followed him as he circled the bronze likeness, absorbing every detail, almost inspecting them as if they were preparing to go on patrol, the dog tag tied into the laces of a worn jungle boot—one around the neck, one in the boot. If they blew your head off, Graves Registration could still ID the body . . . GI-issue towel to wipe away sweat, dirt, and sometimes blood . . . the M-60 gunner, weapon laid across his right shoulder, held in place by a tired hand, twin chains of ammunition crisscrossing his torso. But the eyes . . . troublesome in that they revealed no other emotions than those reflected by their audience. Thornton caught himself as he reached out to grasp one of the trooper's hands. Looking at the others beside him, he realized no one had noticed his gesture. He then understood that there was no fear or self-consciousness in those who came here.

It was time to stand down. The war was over.

Before leaving to rejoin Calvin, he walked the Wall one more time. There was purpose in his step as he searched for the panel marking the year 1965. His first tour of duty. He looked for the names of those he had known. He found them. Ed F. Cockrell—5th Group—killed while advising an ARVN company during a search-and-destroy operation. Charles L. Pickwell—again 5th Group—killed when the helicopter he was riding in was shot down by ground fire. William H. Downing—1st Group—killed in an ambush. There were not many more; '65 had been a slow year. He revisited 1966, then '67.

The faces clicked across his memory's viewer as if in a slide show, except he was the only one watching, the only one present to remember. Moments, gestures, debts, words of advice; they all came again. Billy T. Jackson—point man from the 7th—cut in half when he walked into the muzzle of his NVA counterpart on patrol. Delbert K. Denton—listed as MIA—Thornton had seen his body while the UH-1D attempted to hover near enough for the recovery team to get out . . . intense ground fire driving them off. He knew Denton was dead, but the mission had been executed over a border they weren't supposed to penetrate—no records, no disclosure—the family back home hanging on to a thread that didn't exist. Thornton didn't want to remember any more.

Suddenly it was 1968. The ugliest year of the war. The names beget faces, the faces beget events, the events ended in death. Zapata . . . Barnes . . . Wily . . . He had transferred to SOG at the beginning of his second tour. The missions were hairier than ever; long range and without support. Intelligence leaks began to develop. Teams began to be compromised upon insertion, ambushed by massive enemy units specially trained to run the Soggers to ground and destroy them. He himself had ordered last-minute changes in their insertion points, finding out afterward through agents and prisoners that their primary LZs had been staked out by the NVA.

Rolf T. Johannson. His eyes at first skimmed over the name. Perhaps he hadn't wanted to see it, or maybe he had seen too many he had recognized and wanted no more. But he caught it, the unusual last name triggering an unconscious reaction, moving his hand up to touch the amulet around his throat. Johannson? He had gone back to the World! He was safe! Two tours . . . two damned back-to-back tours! But he was there. Carefully carved into the granite face, quietly reminding his replacement that sometimes you need more than just luck.

"You went back for a third one, didn't you, you crazy bastard," he whispered to himself. "You couldn't stand hanging around Bragg, teaching the young pups, hearing about the rest of us still eating shit out on the trails." His hand tightened around the worn ivory, his thumb massaging the tiny figure as it had since Johannson had given it to him saying, "Remember to rub his belly, Sarge. That's the trick. You rub the fat little fucker's belly and that makes him happy. If he's happy, you're happy." Thanks, Rolf, he thought as he touched his forehead against the cool rock. You were right, my friend. The little fucker brought me home. You were right. . . .

At the end of the day, the caretaker, a young graduate student, completed her rounds of the monument. It was her job to carefully recover all the things the visitors had left at the Wall. She took her job very seriously. It was as if she were a link between those whose names graced the impressive testimonial and those who came to call upon it. What the living left behind she was to care for, in memory of those who had to stay.

As she picked up a carefully folded bush hat, its brim well worn and written upon by an unknown hand, her eye was struck by the tiniest glimmer of something hung in the panel above her. Standing up, she roved the panel from top to bottom, then back again. Halfway up and to her right, she discovered the source of the sparkle. Wedged gently into the cranny that separated one panel from the next was a small ivory statue. It was placed next to the name Rolf T. Johannson, which was the final name inscribed on that particular line.

She carefully pried the jewel out, examining its features once it was safely in her hand. It was an oriental Buddha, expertly carved and set in a tiny throne of gold. The prophet's figure was well worn, his carefully cut lines erased by the constant wear of time. She painstakingly slid her find into a small self-sealing Baggie that she carried for just this purpose. She mused briefly about what the story might be of the man named Johannson and the talisman left behind.

There were so many stories whose endings were known to those she would never meet. . . . That was part of the mystery of the Wall she attended to.

Above her, a helicopter from a nearby military station clattered across the sky. Its rotors drumming out a rhythm that would have been instantly recognizable to those whose names were slowly softening in the evening's light. She gathered up the day's harvest and prepared to leave. The clamor of the helicopter diminishing in the distance was replaced once again by the silence of the park, which was far more gentle in its embrace.

CHAPTER

6

Conrad Billings had been with the DEA for seventeen years. As he sat in the briefing room two floors below his own office, he couldn't help but wonder if perhaps this latest project would alter his plans to retire from the agency. Pulling his cramped frame from the overly padded chair, he strode to the single pot that was on, and poured a cup of what he knew from past experience would be lousy coffee.

Checking his watch, he noted that Bailey would arrive in a few minutes. Their meeting had been set for one-thirty that afternoon, with only Thornton, Bailey, and himself scheduled to attend. Billings didn't expect it to last more than an hour. He had a three-o'clock meeting with the National Security Adviser at his office, which was almost precisely thirty minutes away from DEA headquarters. If Thornton was their man, he'd ask the necessary questions and get the answers he needed within that time. It was actually a cut-and-dried situation when you came down to it; either the former Green Beret would take a shot or he wouldn't.

Privately Billings still wasn't sure he wanted the man to say yes . . . the project was potentially the most sensitive he'd taken part in since he'd joined the agency. The war on drugs had escalated faster than even the most cynical of DEA operatives had predicted, with drug lords challenging them on every front. The money involved was tremendous. A DEA agent started out with a base salary of $22,000 a year, plus benefits. A kid who hustled "crack" could reap that in four good days on the streets. And if the street pusher was dredging in that

kind of money, how much were the suppliers seeing? It bog-
gled Billings's mind to think about it.

Selecting another chair, he sat down to once again study
the graham cracker-colored file containing the guts of M. Sgt.
(ret.) Beaumont Thornton's military career. He'd read it perhaps twenty times already, along with those of several other
candidates the computers had pulled up after the go-ahead to
begin the search had been given. The committee had agreed
on three names, all recent military men, although Thornton
was the only NCO.

Further mission assessments had convinced Billings that
Thornton would best suit their needs. The fact that Bailey had
worked with the man and knew him firsthand made Billings's
selection that much easier to sell. Everyone involved knew the
risks they were taking. Everything had to be absolutely perfect
if Eagle Flight were to succeed. Should Thornton refuse to
participate, it would mean that a total reassessment would
have to be scheduled with the President in attendance. No one
wanted to see a continuation of the scandals that had wreaked
havoc with the Reagan presidency extend into the next admin-
istration.

The sound of the intercom broke his train of thought, causing him to snap shut Thornton's file. "Mr. Billings? Agent
Bailey and a visitor are here to see you." He stood, taking a
moment to straighten his tie and to smooth the beautifully
tailored gray suit coat. He doubted if Thornton would be impressed by his dress, but it didn't pay to look as if he didn't
know how, either. "Send them down please," he ordered.

They had remained silent throughout the drive. Bailey occupied himself by observing the flow of humanity that choked
the sidewalks of downtown D.C., wondering if he'd ever get
his assignment approved to some country, *any* country, in
South America. There was no certainty that Thornton would
take Eagle Flight, and if the project floundered he had to think
about where he might go from Washington.

Thornton sat quietly beside him, his window rolled down
despite the car's air-conditioning going full blast. Bailey had
noted that Thornton was in complete control when they linked
back up that afternoon. The only unusual thing about him was

the length of gold chain carefully wrapped around his left index finger.

After a few more moments Bailey decided that it was time to break the silence. "Hey, what's with the chain? You find it in the park?"

Thornton glanced over at his friend, then down at his finger. "No. It's just something that's been with me for some time now. A friend gave it to me when we were in 'Nam together."

The Camaro picked up speed as they hit a clear stretch of road. Billings wanted them there at 1330, and Calvin knew how the older man felt about his agents being late. He didn't bother to check his watch, knowing that he'd make the appointment with several minutes to spare.

"Any thoughts about what we talked about last night?" he ventured as he pulled into an underground parking lot staffed by two uniformed and armed executive-protection officers. Bailey flashed one of the men his badge while the other ran a mirror fastened onto a long pole underneath the length of their automobile. Bomb threats against the DEA were as common as pigs in Georgia, and no one wanted one driven in by their own agents.

Given the all-clear, Bailey proceeded down the ramp, parking in a slot reserved for him by a number painted on the garage's concrete floor.

Walking to the elevator, Thornton answered Bailey's question with one of his own. "Have you given any thought as to what will happen if this goes sour?"

Stepping into the paneled elevator, Bailey folded his hands across his groin and said, "Sure. It'll mean that there'll be another dive shop opening in San Diego. Only this one will be taught by a professional, instead of you and Hartung." Both men stared at each other, finally breaking into quiet laughter as the doors slipped shut and the elevator began its decent.

When the doors reopened Thornton found himself facing a very stern receptionist. Bailey exited first, once again opening his leather badge case and telling the woman their names as well as who they were there to see. Satisfied with his explanation, the receptionist spoke softly into a miniature boom mike which floated in front of her lips like a meddlesome insect.

Seconds later she motioned both men into the hall, advising them that Mr. Billings was in the third room on their left. Bailey threw her a passable salute. She responded with a very impressive obscene gesture that took Thornton by surprise.

"You two apparently know each other?" he asked as they sauntered down the mauve-colored hallway.

"Yeah, kind of. She used to date a friend of mine until she found out he was also seeing her sister. Now she hates him, and me by association."

"Doesn't seem like a good enough reason to flip you the bird," replied Thornton as they reached the designated doorway.

As he knocked, Bailey coughed a low chuckle before answering. "It's not. I think she's that way because now I'm dating her sister." Thornton rolled his eyes upward to the ceiling, shaking his head at the same time.

From behind the door they heard Billings's voice invite them to enter the soundproofed room.

"Please have a seat. Anywhere will do." Billings stood slightly to the side of the door as they entered, his tone of voice gruff yet friendly. Once inside, he softly closed the door, flicking a light switch that immediately illuminated a sign outside which cautioned that the room was in use.

Thornton made himself comfortable, interested in seeing if the agent would turn out to be another pencil pusher with a good case of the imaginations, or if he was a warrior. Bailey had given no inkling as to Billings's character, probably because the man might end up as his boss. Thornton was thankful he worked for himself these days. Office politics were lost on him. They were a waste of time, effort, and good people.

Billings sat across from them. As the man reached over to open the cover of the file on the single table in the room, Thornton recognized it as his 201. Glancing at the thick document theatrically, Billings spoke. "First off, Mr. Thornton, let me thank you for taking time out of your vacation to visit us. Calvin clarified your time constraints, and I appreciate them. I have no intention of taking up the rest of the afternoon shooting the shit with you. I'll be brief and to the point. Any questions you have I'll try to answer today. Some may have to wait until we know if you're on board or not. In any event, this entire conversation is classified. I don't have to explain that to a man with your background. Nor"—Billings paused ever so slightly before continuing, "do I believe I need to impress upon you the consequences should you decide to share our discussion with anyone."

Thornton studied the man closely. Although he wore his suit well, it was obvious that he preferred casual clothing. His hands were large, padded with thick calluses along their ridges and in the palms. His neck was burned a pecan brown, suggesting months, rather than days, in the sun. Billings's face was the Grand Canyon in human relief, a topographical map of lines, wrinkles, scars, and veins. Searching for a gun, Thornton found no evidence that he wore one. There was no briefcase in the room that might have held a weapon. He concluded that Billings was a field agent, confident in his abilities, secure in his position. There was no hint of a military background in either his language or posture. Career DEA, he thought to himself. A good sign.

"I appreciate your frankness," Bo replied. "Bailey dribbled me enough of what you're considering to whet my interest. No promises, of course, and my memory can be awful at times." Thornton gave the agent his best smile, receiving one in return. They were starting off on the right foot, he thought.

Billings proceeded to carefully outline the background of the problem. He listed options explored by the small group of men charged with determining whether or not there was a solution. Striding around the room, he elaborated on the frustration the group had felt. Bound by laws, impeded by regulations, they had hung themselves like a jury in a bad trial. The President himself broke the deadlock, holding a five-minute meeting at which he pulled out all the stops. Do what it takes, he urged them. Too much was at stake, too many were dying, too much was being destroyed. They had reached a verdict. When he was finished, Billings returned to his seat. The silence in his wake was significant.

"A few questions, if I may?" asked Thornton, breaking the room's quiet.

"Certainly," replied Billings. He reached into his breast pocket, removing a blue silk handkerchief with which he wiped his brow.

"How many others know about Eagle Flight?"

Bailey responded, taking his cue from the senior agent. "With your briefing today there are eleven of us. Five of that number know the entire operation. That group consists of the President, his National Security Adviser, Mr. Billings, myself, and our own director of special operations."

Thornton rose up from his chair, its softness irritating him. "The chairs really do suck, don't they," said Billings. "I personally think they were selected by someone more interested in sleeping through a meeting than listening to what might be said."

Thornton nodded his agreement. "Why use outsiders, regardless of their qualifications? You've got SEAL Eight, DELTA, and FOG, not to mention some damn good people of your own."

Billings spoke this time. He had anticipated the question, impressed that the man across from him was attempting to punch holes in the project rather than jumping at it like some half-starved dog for a piece of meat. They didn't want a cowboy, they needed a professional. "Command-and-control problems. Who runs the team? Does it have a DEA or a military commander? Will the team respond appropriately to a civilian leader? Can the military give up full control over their people? Too many questions, Mr. Thornton, and I might add that you can see the probable answers to all of them."

He could. If they were going to undertake such a project they would have to use independents. By carefully assessing known personnel who had the necessary skills, they could build the right team. "How many others have you talked to like me?" he asked.

"None," replied Billings. "You're it, Mr. Thornton. If you turn us down, that's the end of Eagle Flight. We go back to the drawing board, you go back to finish your vacation."

Bailey left his chair to sit on the edge of the conference table, his feet hanging just slightly above the carpeted floor. "I would be your area specialist, Bo. The mission, equipment, support, funding, it would all come through me. I report only to Billings, and he to the President. It's as tight an organization as we can make it and still be effective."

Thornton turned to Billings. "Why him?" he questioned.

"He knows special ops, he knows you. I know him and his work. You have experience with him from the operations you worked on together in Central America. The package translates as instant trust between us, or as much trust as we can rightfully expect."

Billings paused to check his watch. Bailey took advantage of the break to light a cigarette, exhaling sharply.

Thornton ventured another question at the agent in charge. "Who takes the fall if things get fucked up?"

"I do," sighed Bailey. "If Eagle Flight is blown, DEA will drop the hammer on me. I'll be a junior Oliver North . . . but without the benefit of a starched uniform to wear at the hearings." Bailey blew a perfect smoke ring, jabbing the cigarette through its center, the ring dissolving into a formless cloud.

Billings stood up, tucking Thornton's personnel jacket under his arm like a quarterback taking the snap and going for the end run. "Bo, the drug problem is out of hand. Dealers and suppliers have united so that it is near impossible to root them out under our present system. With their money they can buy better lawyers and post bigger bails. Their weaponry is better than we can provide our own agents. The skills to use that weaponry are being supplied by former soldiers and police officers who are interested solely in the 'Almighty Dollar.'"

"We want to mount one operation. We've targeted a facility and a group of people in the Pacific Northwest who are putting together the largest drug cartel we've seen attempted. If you accept our offer, if the operation is a success, if we can avoid any leaks or disclosures, Eagle Flight just may bring their house of cards down. Right now it all hinges on you."

Thornton felt the meeting come to a close. He broached his final question, half knowing what it was he would hear. "What's the mission?"

Billings glanced over at Bailey, who had retaken his seat. Turning his full attention to Thornton, he spoke quietly, his words a death sentence for men Thornton didn't even know. "The mission has two parts to it. One, the facility must be destroyed. Two, the cartel's members will cease to exist. In short, we want them dead, Mr. Thornton. Stone-cold, motherfucking dead. This is a presidential sanction. Regardless of what happens to Bailey, or to myself, you and your people will be kept out of the picture. If you desire it, we'll have documents to that effect drawn up. The bottom line is this: We're tired of playing by the rules, so we're going to change them, and we want you on our team."

"How much time do I have to decide?"

"Forty-eight hours after you leave here. Once you've made your decision you get in touch with Bailey. Just tell him yes or no. If it's in the affirmative, we'll proceed. If not, just send us a bill for your time."

"You mentioned a team. Who picks 'em?"

Billings tapped the file against the tabletop, sensing that Thornton was leaning toward their position. "You choose your own men. Calvin clears them after he's run their names through our computer. Maximum team strength of three plus yourself. You recommend pay, insurance benefits, and any other compensation you think necessary. I approve that. Anything else?"

By now all three men were standing. "One last question, now that you've raised the issue of funding. Where's it going to come from?" Thornton already had an idea of what he might charge if he chose to accept the mission—and it wouldn't be base pay plus TDY.

Billings lightened the tense atmosphere that had developed over the last hour. "We intend to finance Eagle Flight with the money we've taken off the dealers. Their loss is our gain. No records, no taxes, no reports other than the standard forms required by the agency. Where it goes, nobody knows . . . but us. The funding is there, Mr. Thornton. As long as your fee is reasonable, our coffers are open to you."

Billings checked his watch one final time and moved toward the door. "Gentlemen, I've got a meeting halfway across town. Calvin, please ensure that Bo makes his flight. I believe you two have time for a leisurely dinner before the plane. Bo, I look forward to your call, and I trust this hasn't been a waste of your time." With that, he was gone, the receptionist logging him out as he hurried for his car.

"Well, any thoughts you'd like to share at this point?" asked Bailey as they prepared to leave.

Thornton grimaced at the question. He was being handed a

literal license to kill. For the first time in the country's history, covert operations were being authorized to fight a war within its own borders. A war that was crippling the nation's culture, maiming its best and brightest children, killing its future leaders and developers. He needed forty-eight hours. Not to decide whether he'd accept, but to see if the others he had in mind would join him. Turning to Bailey, he punched the broadly smiling agent hard in the shoulder. "Yeah, where can we get some decent Mexican chow in this town? I'm starved!"

Both men jostled and shoved each other as they headed for the elevator, Bailey turning to deliver a perfectly thrown finger at the now-furious receptionist, who was on the phone and couldn't respond before the doors slammed shut. As he wheeled the Camaro into the gradually thickening afternoon traffic, Bailey ventured a half-question—half-guess to Thornton. "You gonna take it, Bo?" With a glimmer of mischief in his eyes, Thornton turned to the young agent and said, "If I tell you, I'll have to kill you. . . ."

A black pusher who specialized in providing various pills, powders, and *putas* to the power elite of D.C. town was stunned when the red Camaro pulled up next to him. Its two honky occupants eyed his $40,000 Lincoln town car, then pointed their fingers pistol-style at him as the light changed. Crazy fucking city D.C. is, he thought to himself while he confirmed that the nickel-plated .38 he kept under the seat was within easy reach. You never know who's in the car next to you anymore. . . .

CHAPTER

7

The party was in full swing as Anthony "Tony" Dancer graciously began to extricate himself from its vortex. Threading his way through the guests in and around the expansive poolside garden, he gradually moved toward the pink stucco Spanish home he'd named La Casa de Vida. Reproduced from the diagrams of a home built for one of the original Spanish settlers, the "House of Life" was a sprawling two-story affair rumored to have cost the drug czar in excess of 4.5 million dollars. An additional two million had gone into the richly ornate furnishings that graced the home's seventeen rooms, as well as another million in landscaping. The wine red roofing tiles had been made by hand in Mexico, their superior insulating qualities keeping the hacienda's dark interior cool sans air-conditioners, appliances that Dancer despised as being both loud and grossly artificial.

The estate's grounds were surrounded by a combination of wrought-iron fences and adobe walls. Behind the walls lay a network of video surveillance cameras and motion detectors monitored by a specially selected force of men whose loyalty was another possession bought and paid for by Tony Dancer. No one ever entertained the notion of simply "stopping by to visit Mr. Dancer." It was understood that it would be wiser and less unsettling to either receive an invitation, or to call and request an appointment. The Dancer Organization hated surprises. For those who insisted upon them, physical punishment was the normal mode of corrective action.

Dancer appreciated good manners.

Encountering a final group of partygoers before he reached

his office, the man the DEA had targeted as mastermind of the most profitable West Coast drug cartel gladly shook hands with men and playfully squeezed the women who blocked his way. His guests were drawn from a spectrum of the L.A. business community. They were producers, actors, lawyers, doctors, real estate barons, and music personalities. They were his friends, his companions, his associates, and his investors. Through their presence he maintained his respectable front in the community as a successful entrepreneur, a good man to know.

Those friends not attending the private gathering were the men whose business was the same as Dancer's. He was careful to keep a buffer zone between his "doves", as he liked to call them, and his "eagles."

The men not there were his co-authors in the drug trade that had spawned and sustained his rise to power. They were his comrades in arms, his most dependable allies.

Again excusing himself, Dancer slipped between the ornate grand entrance doors that opened into his office, leaving a promise to return soon. Locking the door behind him, he pulled heavy, maroon drapes across the glazed window glass to protect his privacy. Walking quickly across the polished marble floor, the man who controlled nearly sixty percent of the Southern California cocaine and methamphetamine trade went to his desk and pushed one of a series of buttons hidden in its broad expanse.

"I'm in my office. Have the others called yet?"

"Yes they have, Mr. Dancer. I have them all holding for you. Do you want the conference link activated?"

Dancer paused. He moved slowly around the desk, trailing his fingers along its smooth surface, running them over the ever-present clutter of books, ashtrays, Rolodex files, and electronic gadgets which occupied his attentions when he was at work. Settling himself into the plush Herman Miller chair which commanded a view of the entire office, Dancer positioned the intercom's speaker so that it sat at his extreme right front, allowing him to speak in a normal tone while referring to whatever documents might be necessary during the meeting. "Give me just a moment or two, please, then bring us all up on line."

"Certainly, sir. Would you like a refreshment?"

"Perhaps after the call, thank you. Please do ensure every-one outside is having a good time, though, will you?" With his guests' comfort taken care of, he selected another button from the battery at his fingertip and raised a small computer screen from a hidden cavity in the desk's top. Activating it with a series of commands, he brought the required file into view. Labeled Project Alpine, it was the focal point of today's conference.

The red light on the intercom began to blink, alerting him that the participants were ready. Positioning himself so that he could view the screen without difficulty, he acknowledged the insistent light's beckoning with yet another flick of a switch. "Gentlemen," he intoned. "How is everyone today?"

They spoke for nearly an hour. All of the major players were on the line. There was Jerry Graves, representing the Seattle/Anchorage affiliation, Tom Phillips from Portland, Denny "Pointer" LaPoneta from San Francisco, Willy Granger of the San Jose triad, Ralph "Barf Bag" Suddath out of Denver, and Lenny Canolupe, Tony Dancer's man in San Diego.

Winding down the conversation, Dancer began a summa-tion for everyone's benefit. "I think we are all pleased with the progress on Alpine. It appears from what Tom says that we will open as scheduled." He listened to the circle of congratu-lations through the speaker, allowing them time to pat each other on the back. Once an appropriate amount of time had passed, he continued.

"I think we should now discuss, briefly of course, second-ary considerations for Alpine. Any objections?"

LaPoneta from San Francisco spoke up, his voice sounding tinny through the connection. "Yeah. Let's get on with it. I got shit to do, the resort business is well and good, but it don't pay the bills." Hearty laughter erupted from the others.

"Quite right, Denny," replied Dancer as he punched a pro-file of the northern California drug ruler up on the screen. Scanning through the information, he refreshed his memory concerning his closest rival in the trade. Selecting a fact re-cently entered into his data bank, he proceeded to bring Mr. LaPoneta to heel. "Especially when one's bills include a substantial monthly payment to the family of a *very* young 'model' with whom you like to play 'dress-up.'" He heard nothing but the soft buzz of the line until LaPoneta's constricted voice once again made itself present. "You got no right to put that shit out over the line, Tony. What I do in my city is my fucking business!"

The L.A. drug lord smiled at the softly glowing monitor. It always paid to have hard intelligence about your business partners and their activities. It was one of the many aces he held when it came to maintaining his growing influence in various underground markets of his organization. He didn't like to let on how much he really knew about his associates, but sometimes it served a purpose.

"Mr. Canolupe... your assessment on our progress with the lab, please."

Dancer listened intently as his closest associate described final efforts on the secret laboratory being installed in an underground vault beneath the resort's VIP condominium. Once it became fully operational it would be capable of producing and refining over 500 kilos of pure methamphetamine every two weeks. At the projected rate of $16,000 per kilo, that figure translated as an $8,000,000 price tag per shipment. As "meth" or "speed" was one of the top three drugs of choice in the United States, it was a sure mover and definite money maker for those who could supply its users' voracious demand.

"The cookers ran a test load yesterday, Mr. D," concluded the San Diego kingpin, "and everything came out perfect. I've been around this shit for a long time, but I can't remember *ever* putting this high a quality on the streets."

"Excellent," replied Dancer. "What about wrapping and shipping?"

"Cookin' crank is my specialty. Phillips oughta be able to tell you what the wrappers are gonna look like. After all, it's his trucks makin' the deliveries."

Dancer didn't need to prompt the Portland connection's response. Phillips, new to the cartel because of the location of the drug processing and distribution site in his state, was eager to demonstrate his abilities. "We're ready to tag 'em and bag 'em as of the beginning of this week, Tony. I can count on a fleet of twelve over-the-road rigs being available on a twenty-four hour basis. Shipments will be the standard delivery and pickup gig, with only my traffic manager and one senior driver knowing what's actually going down."

"Do we have a storage area available to us?" asked Granger.

Phillips's response was immediate. "Fucking A, OJ. I've arranged for a warehouse along the highway to act as both a staging area and transfer point. In addition, we can use the place for the choppers, should we need 'em to help in the delivery of the goods or whatever else comes up." A murmur of approval sifted through the group as they heard the answers they wanted from their newest affiliate.

Dancer broke in once again, anxious to bring the meeting to an end before they began nitpicking the nuts and bolts of the operation he had been engineering for the last two years. "Security. What's the story there, Mr. Suddath?"

Ralph "Barf Bag" Suddath was the cartel's enforcement arm. With a background that was a murky combination of military, paramilitary, and just plain criminal employments, he was well suited to this assignment. In addition to providing weaponry, personnel, and training for a variety of illegal enterprises, Suddath was also Denver's crown prince when it came to the flow and consumption of illegal narcotics. He was Tony Dancer's kind of man.

"Tony? Yeah, Ralph here. What the fuck you ask about, Tony? I was thinkin' about somethin' else while you all were talkin' to Tom." Dancer imagined the others shaking their heads as he was his. Ralph Suddath was superb in his line of work, but he was limited in his attention span, almost to the point of sounding stupid—which he wasn't.

"Security for the operation, Ralph. We wanted your assessment."

There was a pause during which Dancer imagined Suddath gathering his wits. Definitely a man of action rather than words, he thought. Then Suddath's Texas drawl began to flow through the conference call's line like a slow-moving river of molasses. "My man in Idaho with the White Ring assholes says he's got shooters selected and ready to roll for Alpine. There's twelve all together, reasonably clean records, combat experience in one form or another, and not a doper in the lot."

"How's the fuckin' Nazis feel about losing their best guns, Ralph?" The speaker was Jerry Graves, whose territory included all of Washington State and the civilized areas of Alaska, where he made his home.

"No sweat there. The dude I work with is actually funneling us some of his non-political hitters. His fee is split between himself and the ring. Their boss is only interested in getting hold of additional funding for their defense fund and more guns. For a bunch of looney tunes, they still put business before politics, and they know who's available on the labor market."

Dancer asked who was to be in charge of the security detail once Suddath's team was on site. "Unless you've got objections, Tony, it'll be my man Stennmaker. He's an ex-Navy SEAL with all the qualifications, and he knows his people. Better than that, he's loyal . . . as long as the money's right."

"Any objections?" Dancer questioned his unseen audience. When none were raised, he began to conclude their business.

"That's it, gentlemen. My sincere appreciation for your time, as well as for your efforts. We will look forward to meeting on the twenty-fourth of December at Alpine. I've taken the liberty of arranging a gala opening for the project, so please come prepared to party." There was a round of coarse laughter from the desk speaker as the men acknowledged Dancer's unspoken suggestion that they travel alone to the event. "At the same time we will be making our first shipment from the lab and receiving for distribution a load of a hundred keys from our friends in Colombia. It should be quite a night, my friends, the first of many which will profit all of us equally." Dancer waited for any comments. They were all aware of the meth shipment; that had been part of the original plan. The cocaine had been a side deal by Dancer.

Tom Phillips was the first to respond. "Why the coke, Tony, and how come it's like, uh, you know, a big surprise? That kind of load requires time to negotiate, especially with the Colombians. What the fuck?"

Tony Dancer stood up from behind his desk. Closing his eyes, he envisioned all of them sitting in his office rather than hanging on to their telephones, scenting the air like rats smelling cheese. When he began, his voice was that of a cold steel chisel, each sentence, every phrase hammered home without mercy. He was the Man. They had to know, had to acknowledge that fact.

"My friends," he rasped so slowly that it seemed forever before he finished. "Two years ago I approached each of you on an individual basis. I brought you my plan for a consolidation of our resources, a vision for an organization that could profit all of those involved while protecting our interests at the same time. Our associates in Central and South America have long understood the need for this kind of solidarity. It seemed we should learn from them before they took our pitiful little pieces of turf and made them into one grand empire for themselves." He paused to let them remember his meetings with them, to recall the individual promises made, the arrangements, the collaborations. His throat was dry, making him wish he'd ordered a bottle of mineral water when he'd had the opportunity.

"You're all tough businessmen. But it was a battle royal to convince you my idea had merit, and at the same time I was running my own business, building it up and defending it from the Feds and everyone else who wanted to take me down. Now we are within sight of seeing this thing come into being. Let's not forget our goal, a goal I was the first to set, a goal I wanted to share with my friends."

LaPoneta spoke up, his voice cautious. "Save us the speech, Tony. We all bought off on your plans for a cartel, and we all threw our organizations into the hat; ain't nobody who hasn't heard this story before. But Tom's got a right askin' about the snort, it's not only big fuckin' money up front, but an unexpected risk, given the motherfuckin' Feds' noses up our assholes for the last six months."

Dancer played his trump card, knowing that his role in the cartel was hanging in the balance. The decision to arrange for an additional shipment of coke had been his, but there was more. Instead of 100 keys there were 225. The unmentioned amount was to be diverted to a safe house in L.A. while the rest went to Alpine. He had made some serious commitments to his Los Angeles clients, and had approached the Colombians with the larger deal in order to keep his initial investment down. By paying $13,500 per kilo with an expanded order, he would save roughly $2500 per unit.

That translated into a savings of $312,500 on the original purchase of 125 keys. A substantial amount, given what he was going to move the load for, and ensuring a savings was as meaningful as assuring a profit. By piggy-backing the additional 100 keys onto Alpine, he could distribute it through his friends' systems, allowing them a minor profit while making a killing at his end.

"My friends," he said in his most gracious tone, "I arranged the additional package as a Christmas surprise. Your efforts and cooperation, not to mention trust, has made the Alpine Cartel a reality. Please, please allow me this small token of my gratitude and belief in our combined success."

Again he was assaulted by silence. Then Canolupe spoke up, his words sealing Dancer's manipulations of his supporters like copper pennies on the eyelids of a corpse. "Hey, Tony! You did that for us? Anytime I can make a little extra to pay for the kids' tuition I'm for it, you know what I'm saying? If it's okay with the others, it's fine with me."

They took a voice vote. The decision was unanimous. Tony Dancer had won again . . . and made himself a tidy profit in the process. Dancer ended the meeting with a reminder that all concerned needed to ensure that everything discussed between them remained confidential. As a routine precaution, he had ordered his own phone swept for electronic listening devices every seventy-two hours. He advised the others to do the same if they hadn't already. The conference itself had been scrambled through Dancer's own system, a fact unknown by the participants. He took no chances that weren't necessary, and counting on others was not a part of his game plan.

He was preparing to rejoin the party when the intercom buzzed. "Yes?" he responded, slightly annoyed at his role of host being further delayed.

"Mr. Magnumson is downstairs, sir. He says he's brought a guest that you should meet. Would you like him to wait?"

Dancer rubbed his chin. Magnumson was his personal headhunter, a watchdog over his entire organization. If he was downstairs it meant that he didn't want anyone else to know who this "guest" was. Dancer knew his security chief had

been working on a suspected leak, perhaps he had found it.
"No. Tell him to meet me in the washroom," he commanded.

The "washroom" was located below Dancer's office. He
could reach it by taking the staircase which was just off his
private bathroom at the rear of the office. It was a small
chamber, roughly the size of a toddler's bedroom. There was
no furniture, no shelves. The room appeared to be a large
shower, and in fact a faucet was mounted just off the floor on
the garage side of the room. White bathroom tiles covered
every surface, including the ceiling, and a small fan for venti
lation was mounted in an upper corner of the room. The most
unique aspect of the washroom was the way the floor was
constructed. Built so that it angled down toward the center,
there was a large industrial drain which served to gather refuse
washed into its ever-open mouth. The room was purely utili-
tarian in that it could be cleaned easily and quickly after use.
Its only other feature was that it, like Dancer's office and
bedroom, was completely soundproof.

Magnumson was already in the room when Dancer entered. The heavily muscled security man was in his early thir-
ties, and had learned his trade in the Marines as an embassy
guard. Questionable performance had seen him barred from a
second enlistment, and he had gravitated toward private-sector
work. He had come to the attention of Dancer when assigned
by the agency he was working for to escort the drug smuggler
on one of his Hawaiian holidays.

These days he wore his thick blond hair long, to his
shoulders. His face was devoid of emotion, a carefully constructed mask. His loyalty to Dancer was unquestioned. In the
past, he had killed for his employer, and there was no doubt
he would again if so instructed.

Balled up on the floor at the former Marine's feet lay their
"guest." Dancer squatted down beside the prostrate figure,
keenly interested in what he saw before him. It wasn't very
impressive, he thought to himself. Dressed in a pair of faded
jeans, a black T-shirt, and an expensive leather jacket, the
man obviously was a biker. His hair was long, longer than
Magnumson's, and his face, although handsome, was now
pasty white and strained. He wore no shoes or boots, these

having been removed by his captor as a safeguard against him running too far too fast.

"What's his name?" asked Dancer.

"East. Mark East," replied Magnumson.

Dancer carefully rolled the barely responsive figure over. "Where'd we find Mr. East?" he questioned, peering into the man's clouded eyes, noting they were unfocused yet aware.

Magnumson leaned his bulk against the wall behind him. Reaching into his pants pocket, he removed a small pocket-knife with which he began cleaning his fingernails. His movements were slow, careful, and precise. "He showed up on a fancy Harley from St. Louis about three months ago. Began hanging out with riders from the Free Wheelers, and got asked to prospect for them. Seemed like an okay guy. After a while Deacon began to use him for small jobs, delivering and picking up."

Finishing his nails, Magnumson slipped the knife back into his pocket and squatted down opposite Dancer. Looking down at the hapless character beneath him, he continued. "Old Mark here was one of the four brothers who got picked to escort one of the coke shipments up from Mexico on your boat. He seemed pretty straight, did good work, and kept to himself. Everything was hunky dory until we decided to put him through the test. That's when our 'leak' plugged itself." Jabbing his index and middle finger deftly into the biker's nostrils, Magnumson painfully tilted the man's head back, exposing his throat for Dancer's inspection. With his free hand he pointed to the two needle marks located directly above the jugular vein.

"We shot him up with truth serum twice. The first dose was the standard fix. After what we got, I gave him near double the second time around. He really rattled on after that one." Magnumson laughed at the man's inability to mask his answers. Dancer's preference for drugs to gain information or confirm loyalty had its good points. It was quick, reliable, and clean.

Dancer stood, tired of the game they were playing. The man was either a snitch, a reliable informant, or an agent. In any event he was dead. "So what is he, Mag? A fucking rat . . . or worse?"

Withdrawing his fingers from the man's nose, then giving him a stinging slap across his face before standing, Magnumson answered. "He's DEA, Tony. A friggin' Fed." The man named Mark wriggled in pain and fear as he heard his death sentence spoken. The drug held him in limbo. He could only watch and listen as the two men discussed his imminent departure.

"Pick him up so I can talk to him!" snarled Dancer. Magnumson reached down and, with a forceful yank, snatched the helpless federal agent off the tiled floor. Applying a full nelson so that the man's arms were locked securely above his head, he held the man so that Dancer could look directly into the glazed eyes, rapidly filling up with fear.

"What does he know?" queried Dancer of his hatchet man.

"He knows the pickup point on the Mexican coast. He knows the boat and he knows we use selected bikers from the club as security. He knows you're the sponsor. That's about it, other than the fact that he's a loaner from the St. Louis Feds and his job was to infiltrate the gang and see where it would lead."

Dancer grunted as he took in the information given him. A fucking Fed! De-fucking-A at that! It was standard operating procedure for Magnumson to check out new faces that were involved in shipments and escort duty by running them through a session with the needle. They should have done that before Mr. East had made a trip, but Dancer was wise enough to know that shit happens, and this was one of those unfortunate instances. Killing a DEA agent was not a smart thing to do, but there were no alternatives. "Did he mention anything about Alpine?" whispered Dancer.

Magnumson shook his head no. There was no glimmer of recognition in the drugged eyes of the now-doomed agent. "Good. Mr. East? Can you hear me, Mr. DEA agent?" he asked in an oily voice.

East nodded.

"Excellent! You are a shit-eating rat, Mr. East. You have attempted to compromise my business . . . which of course is *your* business. But I cannot let you go." Dancer moved away from the two men, turning around to stare at them before going on.

"I hope you liked the boat, Mark. My man is going to take you back to it, shove you in a fifty-five-gallon drum, seal the top up, and take you at least six hours out to sea. Then he is going to drop you overboard and watch you sink to the ocean's floor."

Suddenly the calm was broken as Dancer leaped toward the pinioned agent, causing him to struggle backward against the iron grip of his captor. Dancer was shouting now, his control gone, his fury a living thing, fiendish to behold. "The only way to kill a rat is to drown him, you fucking stupid cop! Ever so damn slowly!" Dancer screwed his face directly into the now-convulsing agent's, his breath tainted with the smell of hate he felt for the drugged man before him. He spoke softly, almost cooing the words, his explosion of seconds ago forgotten. "It's a war, Mr. DEA man, a war between your people and mine. In wars there are casualties, which is what you have become. You will be, what is the term, Magnumson? MIA, I believe? Missing in action . . . yes, Mr. East . . . as of today you are missing in action."

Stepping back, Dancer issued curt instructions to the waiting executioner. "No more dope in him from here on out, Mag. I want him aware when his grave opens." The blond mercenary nodded. "I want you to stay out two nights, make it look like you were just out taking a cruise. Go where you like, but draw no unnecessary attention to yourself. Is that understood?" Again the man nodded his assent.

Turning to leave, Dancer stopped and turned one last time to address the fruitlessly struggling agent. "Mr. East, I have a large party to get back to. My people, my friends have no doubt missed me by now. To be a good host is a difficult thing. I'm sure you've thrown enough beer-and-taco-chip gatherings for your fellow narcotics agents to understand my predicament? Please forgive me for not seeing you off, much as I would like to, but I'm sure that Magnumson will afford you every courtesy." With that, the man whose friends' children called Uncle Tony retraced his steps to his office and to the veranda.

As he brushed his hands off on a towel brought by an attentive waiter, he was approached by a leggy starlet whose only accomplishments since hitting Hollywood had been several dish-soap commercials and a frantic round of bed-hopping with anyone she thought could help her break into the business. "Tony," she vamped, "I've been looking all over for you! Is that stud of a bodyguard of yours free for a while? I really would like to spend some special time with him." The girl's eyes glittered with a luster Dancer recognized as amphetamine induced.

"He's handling some business for me right now, my dear. I don't expect him back any time soon."

The woman's eyes fluttered rapidly like miniature gun barrels. Too bad, he thought to himself, a nice piece except for the dope. Dancer himself didn't tolerate his women being involved with drugs, it was too messy and too depressing in the long run. "Huh? Oh . . . sure, Tony, sure. Please tell him to call me any time. My number's listed."

Tony Dancer already knew that. He had everybody's number.

CHAPTER

████████████

8

Two days after arriving back on the coast, Thornton made his call. He was fortunate to find Bailey in his office, catching up on backlogged paper work. Bailey was scarcely able to contain his curiosity.

"What's the score, my man?" he jived. "Are you into it or not?"

Thornton leaned back against the couch, enjoying Bailey's psychic turmoil. Outside it was overcast and cold. The weather a gloomy gray, soulfully highlighted by the wind's somber murmuring through tall coastal pines. "The answer is yes, tell Billings he's bought himself a team leader *if* he agrees to my terms. You ready to copy?"

Billings hustled to find a working pen and some usable paper amid the disaster of his desk. Successful, he returned to the phone. "Send it . . . but slowly. My shorthand sucks." With scrupulous concentration he began to list the things Thornton wanted from the DEA.

"To begin with, I'm going to give you three names. I've talked to each of them, and they're willing to meet with me. They haven't any idea of what the job is, only that it's legal, in-country, and with me in command. Any problems there?"

"None," responded Bailey. "What's their names?" He carefully copied the individual spellings, checking each one as he finished. Satisfied, he asked what was next.

"Funding. I want thirty-five thousand dollars per man. Forty-five thousand for myself as head motherfucker in charge. Each man receives one half his fee upon acceptance of the job, that amount to be sent to his bank via the account numbers I'll provide you. The rest is payable on completion of the mission. If the mission is canceled, the money paid serves as time-and-effort compensation. Got all that so far?" Thornton smiled at the affirmative grunt heard at the other end of the line.

"Insurance. One hundred thousand dollars per man. Make sure all the appropriate clauses are included. Loss of limb, fifteen thousand per. We'll do our own emergency-notification forms once the team's on site. Next comes immediate expenses . . . you still with me, squid?"

"Fuck you," came the reply

"Just checking, glad to see you're still awake. Did I ever tell you that you weren't a bad troop for a Navy dick licker?" Thornton held the receiver away from his ear as a flash flood of profanity roared across the country. When it had subsided, Thornton continued.

"If the job's supposed to take place in the Pacific Northwest, there's no sense in me moving from where I am now. Once Billings approves everything, have fifteen thousand dollars wired out to me. I'll need to rent a house with some acreage around it; one that's fairly secluded and large enough for our needs. There's a few that might fit the bill in the local paper, but I need cash to wrap up whatever fits." Thornton stood up, and after pouring a healthy shot of Jack Daniel's Black into a crystal shot glass, he picked up the phone and dragged it over to the breakfast table. Bailey asked if there was an account they could send the seed money to, and Thornton told him he'd opened one the day before at the local bank. After passing the number to the waiting agent, Thornton asked for an update.

"Billings was favorably impressed, for starters. I met with him yesterday and he said that everything was still a go, providing of course that you agreed to get involved."

Thornton pulled a tender sip of the aged whiskey into his mouth, swirling it around inside, savoring its taste before swallowing. He'd been a Black Jack man for years, his only other alcoholic vice being good imported beers. He seldom drank to excess anymore, although he'd been a hell-raiser when younger. "How soon before you'll have an answer on all this?" he inquired of the disembodied voice in D.C.

"If you'll quit wasting my time and let me off this damn phone, I can probably catch the Man before he goes to lunch. It all sounds acceptable so far. What about service and support?"

Thornton finished his drink and placed the glass neatly on the table. Outside it was starting to drizzle, the waves displaying hoary whitecaps along their peaks as they assaulted the beach front. Several diehard joggers fought against the ceaseless pounding of the wind and spray, their efforts tiny victories appreciated by Thornton as he watched them from his cozy perch.

"We'll have to discuss that once I know what the mission is, and where. I'm sure you guys will be able to come up with whatever we'll need. Right now I'm interested in getting a place to operate from and the team moving. Parallel to that, I'd like to start seeing some hard intel coming from your end, to include a mission date if possible."

"I'll get right on it. From now on out, I'm detached to Billings, no questions asked or encouraged. You gonna be there this afternoon?" Bailey began punching the mission assessment agent's number into another phone on his desk while he awaited Thornton's reply.

"Yeah. The weather is grim today so I'll just be hanging around doing some reading. I may hit the weight room, so leave a message at the desk if you don't catch me."

After hanging up on Thornton, Bailey sat for a few moments, digesting what would have to begin taking place. With Bo on board they could implement pre-mission planning. The logistics so far didn't go beyond what had been expected. He had guessed that Hartung's name would be on the list, and he also knew Sergeant First Class David Lee, currently with the 7th Special Forces Group at Fort Bragg would be included. The third man was an unknown, and he'd run it first. But if this Jason Silver character was anything like the first two, Thornton was definitely putting together a first-class combat team.

After securing his notes of their conversation inside the battleship gray metal desk, Bailey left his office and took the elevator to the floor above his. There he requested access to one of the stand-alone personal computers which was part of a massive data network fed by the mainframe downtown. As he punched in the proper password and code, he wondered why it was taking Billings so long to get back to him. A few more minutes and he was ready to feed the information on Bo's proposed team into the data base waiting to receive it. Within ten minutes he'd have his answer as to the men's security profiles. If they were clean, and if Billings rubber-stamped them after reviewing their hard-copy printouts, Thornton could start recruiting.

Returning to his office with the necessary information and a sigh of relief that everyone entered had come back "Approved," Bailey saw the note ordering him to call Billings's number. Upon doing so he was rewarded with an immediate pickup at the other end. "Agent Billings . . ." announced the strangely stern voice of the man who was now Bailey's mission manager.

"It's Bailey. You called?"

The voice softened as Billings acknowledged the younger agent's identity. "You'd better plan on having lunch in my office, and you ought to be getting your ass over here ASAP. We just got some information about the cartel's plans for Alpine, and the L.A. office has reported one of their undercovers missing."

Bailey was already out of his chair, stuffing his paper work into a day pack and shrugging his Windbreaker on over the holstered .357 on his hip. "Anyone I know?" he asked, hoping that it wasn't

"Agent named East. Was assigned to infiltrate a local biker club suspected of running dope for one Anthony Dancer . . . that shithead's name ring a bell?"

Bailey paused as his mind locked onto the name. East wasn't familiar, but the shithead was. "Fuckin A, I'm on my way, be there in five." With that he was out the door.

Tony "Slimeball" Dancer, he thought as he hurried to his car. Looks like things are poppin' Bo. Hope you're ready to party, because it looks like it's going down.

As Bailey put the pedal to the metal, the intense pressure of 150 feet's worth of ocean depth burst the amateur welds which had been applied to the industrial-strength coffin holding a now very dead DEA undercover agent, jammed tightly inside the metal drum and bloated by two days' worth of body gases. But the bottom tide's constant motion freed the body, which gently swayed and bobbed as the current captured it and began moving the sodden cadaver toward the surface.

CHAPTER

9

Returning from an hour in the Breacon's weight room, Thornton spied his message light blinking, and quickly called Linda downstairs. She was busy checking in a rush of guests, anxious to get started on their weekend away from it all, so she gave him a quick hello and Calvin's brief but concise communiqué.

"Do it."

Checking the time, he was gratified to see that he would probably catch the sergeant major before that afternoon's class if he called right away. Entering the bedroom, he dropped onto the bed and grabbed the nearby phone. After several rings, Hartung's gruff voice answered. "Heavy Hook, it's your quarter, pal!"

"It's me, Frank. Grab a chair. We need to talk."

Several moments passed while Hartung instructed the hired help to man the front, then he was back on the line. "Well, did they buy it or what?"

Thornton smiled broadly. "I just got the green light from Cal. No objections so far, I should see the initial funding arrive within the next two days. In the meantime you need to call Lee at Bragg and let him know he's going to get some unaccounted leave time offered. I'll take care of Jason from this end."

Hartung grunted in the affirmative. If the Army was going to cut one of their own free with nary a fuss, then the level of approval for whatever Thornton was into had to be high. "What should we bring out with us?"

Thornton sat up, swinging his legs off the bed and onto the

thickly carpeted floor. Running a hand through his damp hair, he wiped the accumulated sweat away before it could cascade down his face. "PT clothes—make sure you've got sweats with you, it's been chilly out—and a coupla sets of civilian clothes, nothing too fancy. No handguns, period. If anyone has a preference, I'll order it. We'll be getting some range time in, anyhow, so we can zero then. A blade's okay, just make sure it's checked through with your cargo luggage. Other than that, everything else will be provided."

"Roger that!" answered Hartung. "Now, when do you want everyone up there? It's going to take me at least seventy-two hours to close the shop down. I can have the boys take care of the classes; they just need the keys and schedule."

Thornton began calculating his next moves. They needed a forward operating base (FOB), transportation, phones (that meant a scrambler from Bailey's end, and probably a pager for each man on the team), some basic household items, as well as mission-prep gear to begin planning and rehearsing the operation.

"Frank?"

"Yeah, Bo."

"You and Lee will need the most time, so don't sweat getting here for at least five days. I can get Silver airborne ASAP; he'll work with me on supplies. By the time you and Lee hit town we should have the basics in place. Does that work for you?"

"Yeah, shouldn't be a problem. If Lee gets his orders cut fast enough he may just beat me out there."

Thornton nodded to himself. "That wouldn't bust my balls. The way this thing's shaking out, we'll probably be on a short count, anyhow."

It was Hartung's turn to be silent. He gazed around the shop he had grown to love and wondered if he ought to remind his best friend that they now had something more than just their asses to lose. "Hey, Bo, mind if I do a little thinking out loud?" he asked.

"Shoot."

"I know you couldn't pass along all the poop when you called, but I've been around long enough to know that this sounds like it has Uncle Sam's name written all over it."

Ensuring that the door to his office was securely shut, Hartung continued. "We've got a good deal here with Heavy Hook. Hell, we're making money like it's going out of style, and if next year is anything like this one you'll be able to get that house you want up there *without* worrying about getting your nuts shot off."

Thornton listened. He knew what the old Indian fighter was saying was true. They—he—didn't need this shit anymore. But there was more to it than just the money or the excitement of doing what he knew best with men whose capabilities and skills defined the term "elite." It was the purpose, the goal. He didn't have any kids, might not ever have any, for what it was worth. But if he did, he sure as hell wouldn't want them destroying themselves on the poison the vermin calling themselves "businessmen" sold.

Maybe he wasn't a judge who had the power to sentence, or a lawyer who could bring them to trial . . . and he sure as shit wasn't ever going to wear a badge. But he could be something that would have an immediate impact as well as a lasting effect on those whose trade was misery and degradation.

He could be the last thing they'd see on earth.

"Frank, have you ever heard the term 'techno-commando'?"

Hartung laughed. "Nope. Can't say that I have . . . sounds like one of them cartoons the kids watch these days, though. Why?"

Thornton lay back down on the bed. For just an instant he wished for a cigarette, wanting the relaxing euphoria a good smoke could provide at times just like this one. He'd quit two years ago after realizing what he was doing to his body. Pushing the urge away, he continued. "A techno-commando can be either one individual or a team. The concept being that we've accelerated the technical end of warfare to the point where we can now outfit small groups of men with the kind of firepower that used to be available at the company and battalion level. On top of that, there now exists a level of sophistication in communications, radar, laser systems, and night-vision devices that can arm these groups with a lethality factor before unheard of."

"That's all well and good, Bo. But unless your 'groups'

have the savvy and training to use all that super-shit, you might as well give it to a bunch of monkeys. Hell, you've seen that in the line units they field these days!" countered Hartung.

"True. That's what I'm getting at. For the techno-commando to be effective, it must employ only the best of personnel. They have to be highly trained, motivated, independent, while still adhering to the team concept, and dedicated toward mission accomplishment. Add the most sophisticated equipment and support systems to this caliber of soldier, and you've got one devastating option available to you."

Hartung pushed his chair back so he could get his booted feet atop his desk. Once comfortable, he fired another question at Thornton. "So what the fuck does this techno-disco shit have to do with the DEA?"

Thornton was excited. He had felt something like this was coming even before he retired. A constant reader, he'd stumbled onto the concept he was discussing with Hartung in several recent books. The more he verbalized his thoughts with the sergeant major, the more he felt he knew what might be taking place.

"Forget the DEA a minute. Now you and I both know that politically there isn't a major power, ours or theirs, that's going to resort to dropping a nuke any time soon, right?"

Frank sighed. His boy was on a roll and he knew Thornton wouldn't let him off the phone unless he let him finish. "Yeah, no surprises there."

"The fact is that we can't deploy our major combat units anymore. Especially if the trouble is being incited by guerrillas or terrorists. Take El Salvador for instance. Shit, we were duty bound not to exceed more than fifty-five military advisers...."

"Trainers!" interrupted Hartung.

"Yeah, right. Trainers. Anyhow, the point is that with all the high-speed reaction forces and equipment available to our politicians, they can't utilize it. A terrorist squad takes an airliner, what do we do? Sure as hell we don't send in the Marines. A known assassin drops a head of state from twelve hundred meters, how do we react? It's not with a B-52 strike against his capital city. But we have to do *something*. Because if we don't, then the bastards can and will walk all over us."

Hartung began to get the picture. "Are you saying that the DEA is forming one of these sci-fi commando teams to mess with the dopers?"

Thornton chortled. He knew Frank was playing dumb. Hartung's thirty-year career included both active and passive associations with most of the elite outfits the services had fielded during his time in uniform. In addition he'd been an exchange student with the British SAS, perhaps the closest thing to the techno-commando concept currently practiced by a conventional military establishment anywhere in the free world.

"What I think, is that someone very high up in our political system has begun to at least listen to the beat of a new and different drummer. A techno-commando unit could be formed and launched against *any* threat, either foreign or domestic. The sponsoring power could compose its personnel and equipment configuration with a specific target in mind, and disband it immediately after the mission's completed. It could be inner service, or independent of any service. The team would never have to know who they were working for, and diplomatically the results of their actions could be denied by the sponsor, with little fear of discovery or leaks."

"So instead of big battalions with their big guns, this 'sponsor' would be sending out almost totally independent hunter-killer teams like the LRRPs," exclaimed Hartung as he caught the same excitement Thornton was feeling.

"Exactly!" pumped Thornton. "But they'd be better than the LRRPs, better than SOG even. Minimal command-and-control considerations. The team would have access to all the intelligence sources possible as well as material support. Only a select group at the top, made up of seasoned players, would know the scope of the operation under way. Anyone else involved simply supplies what they're told to without question. It's the perfect blind operation, sans political constraints or public awareness."

"It's spooky," said Hartung.

"It's weirder than spooky," offered Thornton. "It's what I think we're into if Jason and Lee agree to play."

Hartung stood up. He still wasn't sure what the program

was about, but he could wait until they were somewhere secure before passing judgment on what Thornton was saying. "I just want to be sure you know what you're getting into, Bo. We've both been around long enough to know that those dumb bastards at the top will do and say anything if they think it'll serve a purpose. I'll tell you one thing right now, if the CI-fucking-A has any part in this, I'm out. I've seen them fuck up a wet dream too many times in too many places to give them another shot."

Thornton laughed. "I hear you, Frank. Believe me, I'm not interested in working around those folks again myself. But I don't think this is their action. It's too select, and the players I've met so far are too rough around the edges. But I agree with you, the first smell of the Agency and I'll be back at Heavy Hook before you miss me."

"Airborne and Amen," Hartung replied.

"Okay, then. You pass the word to Lee and I'll get Jason's reservations set up. Let's plan on talking in three days, unless something major pops. Oh, you can do me a favor."

"Name it."

"Grab my Randall, the number-two, and UPS it up to me tomorrow. All I've got with me is the Russian piece, and it's strictly backup."

Hartung quickly jotted down Thornton's address. He was the only man alive who knew what "the Russian piece" was. When Thornton had been assigned to the battalion in Panama, he'd been detached for a special assignment, thought by most to be back at Bragg. In fact the multilingual sergeant had been ordered into Afghanistan to train the "Muj" in how to effectively raid and ambush their Russian opponents. While accompanying one of the Mujahideen units during an ambush (something Thornton had been ordered to avoid, but typical of his commitment to whoever he was working with), they had run into a squad of Russian paratroops on patrol. During the ensuing firefight, Thornton had gone hand to hand with one of the Russians, finally killing the man with his Randall stiletto.

While searching the body, Thornton discovered a spring-driven combat knife that he recognized as being an issue item to the Soviet Spetsnaz, or special forces. Shaped like a jawa stick, the knife consisted of four individual parts which fit together to form the whole. An industrial-strength spring served to propel the knife's blade from the handle once the trigger mechanism was depressed. A tubular extension fastened to the rear of the blade provided stability during flight. The sheath was another tube, the end blunted so that the weapon could be used for nonlethal strikes if so desired.

Hartung had watched Thornton demonstrate the knife after his return from Afghanistan. The blade had easily penetrated half-inch plywood, and both men recognized it as being an awesome close-combat weapon. Only the sergeant major knew Thornton had the dagger, a weapon he called a "springblade."

Hartung knew that Thornton practiced regularly with the springblade. He'd even gone so far as to have several spare blades custom-forged by Texas knifemaker Jack Crain. The Green Beret sergeant was so adept at firing the weapon that Hartung had witnessed full-depth penetrations of the razor-sharp blade at up to thirty feet. Thornton referred to the knife as his "final option," a last means of defense when all else failed. "You hit someone with that thing and you'll fuck up his day, Sarge," Hartung told his friend after observing one particularly spectacular shot the knife-wise veteran had made.

"Better him than me, Frank," was Thornton's response.

Frank agreed. The springblade was nothing to fuck with, nor was the man who wielded it. Both dealt in quick and violent death, although death at Thornton's hand was death well deserved. The man was neither a head case nor cruel. He was a professional soldier, perhaps the best Hartung had ever seen. There was nothing John Wayne or Rambo-like about Bo Thornton, and there was no other man Frank Hartung would rather have at his side when the shit started flying and men started dying.

Bo Thornton would stand, come hell or high water, you could bet a year's jump pay on it.

CHAPTER

10

Ten days later Calvin Bailey stood in the living room of the house Thornton had found for his team. The men themselves were scattered about the room. Jason Silver had arrived the week before, immediately taking on the awesome task of predicting and arranging for the team's needs, while Thornton searched for a base of operations. At five feet eight inches tall, he was the smallest man on the team. His coal black hair was fashionably long, and he wore reading glasses when working. Bailey knew Silver carried a long, deep scar across his lower belly, a reminder of his clash with NVA ambushers. What struck Calvin most about the spunky ex-LRRP was his ability to work around Thornton as if he were reading the man's thoughts. The two were definitely a "Mutt and Jeff" team. Silver playing off the big man's character so that even in the most serious situations, everyone seemed to have a smile at hand.

Seventy-two hours later, David Lee had flown in from Bragg. A lean, powerful man, Lee personified the term "paratrooper." With slate-gray eyes, strawberry blond hair, and the features of a male model, he was easily the most handsome of the group. Underneath his pleasing appearance, though, there beat the heart of a Viking warrior, natural considering the man's Nordic heritage. His very puzzled battalion commander had handed him the Top Secret—NOFORN orders personally, then wished him well. Hartung arrived last, his concerns for the shop taking an additional day's attention before he'd been satisfied they'd have something to come back to.

Not bad, Bailey reflected to himself. A crackerjack combat team put together in less than two weeks, their base functional, and everyone just waiting for me to fill them in on what the hell happens next.

Bailey sat at a large wooden table which dominated the room. In front of him were dossiers on each of the men Thornton had gathered. Opening the first one, he began to review their backgrounds, correlating each man's face in the room with the photo provided. One of the things that would sink you faster than shit was to forget a man's name, or worse yet, call him by someone else's during an initial briefing. It meant you hadn't done your homework, or that you didn't care about your people. Bailey had, and he did.

Frank Hartung—thirty-year man, United States Army. Fought in both Korea and Vietnam. Highest award was a Distinguished Service Cross he'd gotten in Korea while with General Bowen's 187th Airborne Regimental Combat Team, after their jump into Pyongyang. Hartung had gone into Vietnam in 1957 to train the core of the South Vietnamese Ranger program. From there he'd spent time flying in and out of several different Southeast Asian countries, finally ending up back in Vietnam, where he became part of the original SOG program. Assigned to Command and Control North (CCN), Hartung had been NCOIC of the Krieg project. Krieg teams were responsible for ultralong-range reconnaissance missions as well as selected target interdictions. Their boundaries were limited only by their available method of insertion. Thornton had been the one-Zero for RT Python, Krieg's only HALO/SCUBA detachment. Together, the two men had made an unbeatable combination. The retired sergeant major was an expert in special operations and its requirements.

Sergeant First Class David Lee—Lee had joined the Army in 1974, after two years of college. He'd served his first tour with the 25th Infantry Division in Hawaii, making buck sergeant in three years. His second enlistment took him to Georgia, where he attended Ranger school. One year later, Lee volunteered and was accepted for the then newly formed antiterrorist unit called DELTA. Eighteen months later he requested a transfer to Special Forces, which was granted. Upon completing the Special Forces qualification course, Lee was assigned to the 7th Special Forces Group as a light-weapons specialist. The 7th further assigned him to their forward battalion in Panama, which was supporting efforts in both El Salvador and Honduras.

During a military training mission to El Salvador, Lee was wounded when his troops clashed with a unit from the FMLN. He was awarded the Purple Heart. Upon his recovery, Lee joined one of the battalion's two sniper detachments . . . whose team sergeant happened to be one Master Sergeant Beaumont "Bo" Thornton. Lee was considered one of the top three snipers in the Army, and was currently assigned as a senior instructor to Special Operations Target Interdiction Course (SOTIC) at Fort Bragg.

Jason Silver—Silver had served twenty-two months in Vietnam. His first tour had been with Company E, 58th Infantry (LRRP) in 1968. During May of that year he was severely wounded in an NVA ambush, and flown to Japan for treatment. Upon recovering, Jason was told that the nature of his injury was severe enough to keep him from returning to combat. Instead of accepting his ticket home, the young recon man requested reassignment to his old LRRP company, and upon his return was assigned to the unit's intelligence shop. It was here that he met Staff Sergeant Thornton, who was recruiting volunteers for the Krieg Project. The men became fast friends, with Silver constantly on the lookout for both men and information that might benefit Thornton's operations.

Silver was a first-rate intelligence analyst, leaving Vietnam with two Bronze Stars for valor, a Purple Heart, and a ream's worth of recommendations for Officer Candidate School. Choosing to leave the Army rather than become one of its officers, Silver returned to school, where he graduated with a B.A. in computer science.

A little-known fact about the wiry LRRP was that he had trained with the 5th Special Forces Group at their recon-commando school in Nha Trang as an explosives expert. Currently Silver ran his own industrial-demolitions firm in New Mexico.

Bailey sat back after completing his review. Looking around the room, he was aware that he was the youngest of any of the men present, although Lee was only two years older than he. They were talking quietly amongst themselves, waiting for Thornton to introduce the agent who would be their mission link. Bailey marveled at how ordinary they all appeared. But given a situation that demanded their hard-earned skills, these "ordinary"-looking men would become a formidable force. He was proud to know them, and proud to be one of them.

Thornton entered the room, his presence starting a chain reaction of uplifting faces and swiveling eyeballs. "Gather 'round, gentlemen," he said. "I've got someone to introduce to you. So let's give him our undivided attention."

One by one they scooted their chairs forward until they were seated in a rough semicircle around Thornton and Bailey. Thornton began, "This is Calvin Bailey. He's DEA and our area specialist for the mission. I've known Cal since '84, when we salted a Nic port with some anti-ship mines. He's a former SEAL and has seen his share of shit. I trust him, which means you can, too. Cal . . ."

Bailey was left standing alone as Thornton took a seat next to Hartung. "Gentlemen," he began, "what we have in mind is basically a raid. The primary target is a drug lab which, if it is allowed to go into operation, will produce massive amounts of methamphetamine, or 'speed.' The facility is also meant to serve as a shipment point for other narcotics to include cocaine and heroin. It will be your job to prevent any of this from taking place."

After pausing for a moment, satisfied that he had their attention, Bailey continued. "In conjunction with the lab's destruction, you will be tasked to isolate a group of identified drug czars who will be present to 'open' their new business interest. Once you've accomplished this, they are to be terminated. This is a Presidential sanction."

He watched as eyebrows were lifted around the group. Silver was the first to speak. "By 'terminated' you mean that we're going to whack these dealers, right?"

"Correct," answered Bailey.

Thornton glanced at the group. "Any objections to that portion of the mission?" he asked. One by one the men shook their heads in the negative.

"When's this supposed to go down?" asked Lee.

Bailey turned his attention to Thornton, who hadn't been told of the date yet himself. "Our information is that the lab will be open for business as of the twenty-fourth of December. That's when we want to hit it."

Hartung grunted at the news. "Christmas Eve? Shit, this is gonna make it kinda hard on Santa, isn't it?" A low rumble of laughter rippled across the room.

Bailey pressed forward, sensing that the mood had shifted from the speculative to the accepted. "The lab has been 'buried' under the cover of a large, ultra-fashionable vacation resort called Alpine Manor. It's situated at the base of the Cascades in central Oregon. We've got the resort's complete layout, thanks to the state, where the plans had to be filed for approval. In addition, we believe we've isolated the building that the lab is located in."

"How about photos of the targets?" asked Hartung.

"I've brought a complete briefing package with me. In it you'll find a general description of the operational area, the DEA's concept of the mission, an area study, our current intelligence update, assets that are available, and the location of the mission support site. It'll be up to you to develop your own operation and training plan, requests for equipment, pre-mission rehearsals, and contingency plans."

The men all nodded their approval. Good planning depended on relevant and confirmed intelligence. They wouldn't consider stepping one foot outside their coastal hideaway unless they felt that they had the highest degree of success offered to them. With what Bailey had brought, they felt ready to commit to the next phase.

Thornton stood, indicating to Bailey that he could relax for a moment. The agent acknowledged the older man's authority and returned to his seat at the table.

"Okay, listen up, everybody. First off, if any of you wants to *di-di*, this is the time. No problem, if that's your decision. This is heavy shit we're getting into. If you've got questions about being a part of this team, then say so now. I personally wouldn't think less of anyone who wanted out. We've all done our share and then some, and everyone except Dave is a civilian at this stage of the game." Thornton checked the group, their eyes on him as he observed each man for the slightest indication of doubt. Finding none, and getting no takers to his offer, Thornton continued.

"Assignments. Everyone's gotten a chance to either renew old ties or get introduced, so I won't play 'welcome wagon.'

Silver has been handling logistics since his arrival, and you can thank him for all the comforts of home." Jason stood, performing a deep bow to the applause of his teammates. Thornton continued. "Frank, you've got operations and training. Get up with Calvin and let him know what you want for the base here." Hartung nodded, then stood and moved over to where Bailey sat.

"David?"

Their only active-duty Green Beret looked up from a photo Bailey had handed him. "You'll determine our armament and training. Get a dream sheet together of what everyone thinks he might like to have, and pass it by me. Jason will be responsible for the demo stuff, so don't concern yourself with that end of it."

"Everyone will be responsible for his own physical conditioning. The only training we'll take together will be an hour's worth of hand-to-hand every afternoon. Wake-up will be at oh six hundred from now until we go into final prep. You can run, use the bikes in the garage, or swim. I've made arrangements down at the Breacon for us to use their weight room. The key will be hanging in the garage. If anyone asks who you are, just tell them you're a guest of mine, as I'm keeping my condo there for off-site meets."

Realizing it was time for lunch, Thornton raised his hands to capture their attention one more time. "Bailey, Frank, and I will be the command-and-control element. Expect a team meeting every morning at oh eight thirty, every afternoon at thirteen hundred, and in the evenings when necessary. We have three weeks before launch. That means we're on a short count. We can't afford any wasted time or effort, so do it right the first time around. Maintain a low profile when you're in town. My only hard rule is that no one hits the booze from here on out. I won't tolerate a drunk or an incident brought on by one. Is that understood?"

The men signaled their understanding. They'd all seen teams destroyed by alcohol.

When the meeting broke up, Calvin motioned for Thornton to join him. The two men walked across the hardwood floor and out onto the balcony that overlooked Oregon's windswept coastline. The view was spectacular. Looking at Thornton,

Bailey spoke. "They took everything pretty well. It was almost too easy in some ways."

Thornton replied, his eyes on a sailboat whose prow was slashing its way through the choppy waters as it headed north toward Seaside. "Remember, you're working with professionals, Cal. These guys have been over the mountain and seen the bear a hundred times; all you're offering is another trip along a different path."

"You think three weeks is long enough for what we have to do?" Bailey was now watching the boat, imagining himself on its foam-drenched deck as he struggled to keep the main sail taut.

"If the red tape is kept to a minimum . . . if we can get the equipment we ask for . . . if your intelligence is good . . . if we're kept to the original launch date . . . if all that and everything else works in our favor, then I'd say that three weeks is reasonable."

Bailey sighed as he reached for a smoke. Reasonable, he thought. Three weeks to mount a major operation whose very nature was a response to the unreasonable.

Snapping his lighter closed, he once again envisioned East's body on the table. The swollen and ravaged corpse had been spotted by a freighter several days after the narc's disappearance. It was brought in under a John Doe listing. The DEA had squashed any news of its recovery, not wanting to alert Dancer and perhaps compromise those others they had scattered throughout his network. An errant raindrop struck the cigarette's tiny glimmering coal, forcing Bailey to take several deep drags in order to keep it alive. Looking sideways at Thornton, the ex-SEAL's features took on a brutal appearance which betrayed his inner emotions. "Like you said, Bo, we got no time to waste. Tell me what we need and I'll get it for you. Come the twenty-fourth I want see Tony Dancer and his asshole buddies buried under the Christmas tree, instead of decorating it!"

"Ho, ho, ho," snorted Thornton as he turned for the sanctuary of the open door.

The rain succeeded in suffocating Bailey's cigarette before he could get inside.

CHAPTER

11

A week passed. The men leaned into their individual assignments with a fervor that encouraged Thornton. Hartung and Bailey headed into Portland the morning after their meeting. With them, they took a shopping list of supplies and materials necessary for the team's pre-mission planning. When they weren't either working out or engrossed in planning sessions, the sergeant major and Bailey committed themselves to the construction of the team's tactical operations center. The house Thornton had rented had a second floor with connecting bedrooms, a large den, and a full bath. It was the perfect format for their TOC.

Each operative was assigned his own room as a combination workplace and living quarters. He was provided with pens, pencils, writing pads, and other administrative items to prepare his portion of the mission. Any specialty items were ordered through either Bailey or Hartung. In addition to their work needs, the rooms were furnished with bedding, a cot, two footlockers, and a double file drawer to secure papers. Hartung converted the den into a briefing room and communications center. Bailey installed two telephones and the scrambler device sent out by Billings, as well as a FAX machine. They now had secure voice- and document-transmission capabilities. Anything needing to be shipped would come through either Federal Express or UPS. Their weapons and munitions would be brought in by Bailey, who would pick them up from a secure drop site in Portland. To prevent too much interest to their presence and activities, the windows throughout the TOC were hung with heavy black blinds like those found in amateur darkrooms. This allowed the team to work late without arousing the slightest suspicion on anyone's part, including that of the local constabulary.

For all anyone knew, they were just another group of tourists with too much money and free time on their hands.

The night the TOC was christened, Bailey complimented Hartung on his work. "Frank," he told the man after they'd hooked up the commo equipment and tested it, "you're good enough to have been a SEAL if you hadn't screwed up and joined the Army."

Hartung turned a distressed eye on the grinning DEA agent, his face a mask of simulated pain at what he'd just heard. "You can forget that frog shit," he growled. "If God wanted Frank Hartung to go to sea, he would have issued him gills and webbed feet! Now cut the crap, squid, and get the others up here so they can see what those of us who've been working have accomplished."

The others were impressed.

It was nearing four o'clock when Thornton, dressed in his sweats and tennis shoes, ordered them outside for hand-to-hand. The men catcalled to each other as they changed into their "fightin' clothes," as Lee had nicknamed them, then trooped downstairs and out into the fenced backyard, where Thornton had marked off a large circle with engineer's tape. As Thornton moved into the center of the ring, the others took up positions around its circumference. Held in his hand was a long black rubber knife modeled after the legendary Applegate-Fairbairn-Sykes commando dagger. Specially designed and manufactured by Al Mar Knives, it was the finest training aid Thornton had found to teach close-quarters combat. Each man on the team had been issued one after Hartung and Bailey returned from their shopping spree.

"Listen up!" barked Thornton. The team fell silent, clowning forgotten as they prepared for the coming instruction. "We spent most of last week concentrating on basic falling techniques, rolls, and recoveries. You all look pretty good, and the sergeant major tells me that your individual PT efforts are fairly impressive." The former One-Zero gazed approvingly at the men, nodding his head in silent acknowledgment of their efforts.

"This week we begin working with the knife. There's two reasons why I feel it's important. The first being that while checking your personal gear I noticed that everyone brought a blade with him. If you're going to carry a combat knife on this mission, *I'm* going to know that *you* know how to use it." As he was speaking, Thornton began maneuvering his blade, deftly switching grip styles as if the knife were an anatomical extension of his hand. One by one, the men's attentions were drawn to the steadily moving black blade. Each of them secretly wondering when Thornton would miss a beat and fumble the knife in front of them.

Jabbing the dagger's blunt rubber tip at the man nearest him, Thornton grinned. "I'm not going to drop it, asshole." They all began to laugh, their embarrassment quickly forgotten as Thornton continued. "A more important reason is that all of us have been out of action for at least a year or two. The exception being David, of course." Their eyes focused on the team's only active-duty member, whose last assignment had been the removal of a Cuban sniper team operating along the Guatemalan border. It had been one of Lee's best shots, nearly 1500 meters' worth, using a .50-caliber system recently adopted by the Special Operations Command's sniper teams.

Lee kept his eyes on Thornton.

"There's no quicker way to peel the bark back than to hook it up belly to belly, blade to blade. By the time we launch out of here I want that civilized veneer we've adopted removed. When you come face to face with the bastards we're going up against . . . you won't think twice about ramming a length of steel through him, or atomizing his spine on full auto!"

Thornton selected Silver, inviting the former LRRP into the center circle with a steady waving motion of his knife. Jason began complaining as he stepped forward. "How come I always end up being the pivot man for these circle jerks?" he whined.

"'Cause you're short, little man . . . and God hates short people," taunted Hartung from a chair on the porch.

"Hey, Bo! What about that old bastard?" Silver demanded. "Why isn't his nasty ass out here . . . ?"

Before Thornton could respond, Hartung did. "Two reasons, stud. The first being that any man who's stupid enough to pull a shiv on me is gonna get center-punched with thirteen nine-millimeter motherfuckers from Mr. Browning's Hi-Power. Number two is that this 'old man' is going to be flying covey for you bozos. The only thing I need to worry about is bringing along enough hot coffee to keep me awake while you're playing Rambo-commando with our doper friends."

Silver turned to shake his rubber dirk at his tormentor, abruptly falling to the ground when Thornton delivered a not-too-gentle side kick behind his left knee. "Never take your eyes off your opponent," Thornton intoned while Jason picked himself up, the effort accompanied by Hartung's insistent cackle. "You break contact and your ass is dead. Remember that. What we do here is what we'll do on the ground, so let's quit screwing the pooch and get to it."

The embarrassed LRRP pulled himself together and turned to face Thornton. "Sorry, Bo, you're fucking-A right. Let's do it."

Thornton put them through the ringer for the rest of the afternoon. They didn't practice the in-quartata, nor did they adhere to any particular system or doctrine. Instead they learned to hide the knife along the inside of their forearms, its handle grasped tightly in the palm of the hand, the blade pointing up. Surprise and deception were their allies. Never telegraph your intentions, Thornton admonished. With your man in close, deliver a roundhouse slash deep into his throat or face, then follow it up with reverse plunging attacks into the stomach. Blow his nervous system out, leave his senses shredded, fuck him up!

Using Silver as a demonstrator, Thornton illustrated his by-the-balls philosophy as he slowly went through the moves he had described. After each step he paused, pointing out the locations of the various arteries, veins, and muscle junctures which were their primary targets of attack. Finished, he then paired them up to practice, watching as they rapidly gained their confidence back, becoming once again predators of their own kind.

During breaks he lectured them. His keen observations were interwoven with years of study and the seasoning of three kills he himself had made with his hand-forged Randall. Remember, he cautioned them, you've got no more than thirty seconds once it begins. Knife fighting doesn't happen much anymore. Knifework's either going to be a pre-planned action, an unexpected encounter, or your last resort. You're going to have to react quickly—seize the offensive—and keep on truckin' once your man's down. Fuck the pretty-boy shit. Rip his ass and let him bleed.

They all listened, their senses and emotions backsliding to a more primitive state as they recalled their own encounters along the trails and in the jungle's deepest holes. Thornton conjured up long-buried impressions of wet, steamy blood splotches on their faces, hands lubricated by sweat and human grease, the rising of their hackles as their quarry (or their hunters?) pressed closer, looming larger in their gunsights or nearer to their unsheathed blades.

With each description he stripped away the yogurtlike putty of civilized man. With every instruction he replaced it with the singular intent of the professional warrior. He didn't have to work too hard. Like the sculptor whose statue was under all the excess stone that he merely chipped away, Thornton's legion was comprised of old campaigners whose characters had been forged on the anvil of battle. He needed only to burnish off the patina that covered their true natures.

By the end of the second week they were hunters once again.

CHAPTER

12

They sat around a low table that had been fashioned from a cable spool thrown away by the phone company. It was the same with much of the furniture that littered the room. Old and mismatched, the decor was a combination of Salvation Army turn-downs and garage-sale castoffs. It was a room whose spills and stains were a combination of the edible, the drinkable, and the biological.

The biker known as "the Monk" was flanked on either side by his most trusted advisers. He had earned his dubious office by the use of his fists, boots, and a Neanderthal political intuition. At six eight and 275 pounds, his word was law amongst the group of riders which made up the membership of the Satan's Rebels motorcycle club. Today he and his lieutenants were meeting to discuss a crisis which was threatening the club's economic livelihood.

Nazi Bill was just finishing a beer. Around his head he wore a black band with the emblem of the German SS embroidered in its center. He was exceptionally lean in appearance, his clothes accenting his saplinglike frame. He served as the club's vice-president as well as armorer. "We damn sure gotta do somethin', Monk!" he complained. "The word on the streets is that Dancer and his people are going to start bringing in shitloads of meth at damn near three-quarters what we're moving it for. That happens and we might as well kiss our sales good-fucking-bye!" The agitated biker grabbed a lukewarm beer from the table, popping its top and draining half of it before slamming the can down.

"Whadda you hear, Roadrash?" asked the Monk, his eyes

buried beneath thick black brows which had grown together to form a hairy bridge between his eyes.

"Same shit Bill's sayin', Monk. Our own fucking people are jackin' their jaws that they'll start buying from Dancer's assholes if the product's good and the price is lower. I talked with two of our cookers up in Oregon, and they say they're hearin' about a new lab going in somewhere up by the mountains. Supposed to be a high-tech operation with some expensive talent doing the mix." The speaker called Roadrash leaned forward like a man with a dirty secret who doesn't want to be overheard sharing it. "I also hear that our brothers in the White Ring are supplying the gunners for this lab. . . ." He sat back, his eyes glittering as he watched their expressions deepen with the impact of his news.

"Ain't nothing new there," murmured the fourth member of the group. "We all know the Ring's into politics and nothin' else. If they can make some bread pulling security for a shit-for-brains outfit like Dancer's, they'll do it. We all know they got a lot of their own doin' time in the pen . . . and good lawyers cost."

"Fact!" growled the Monk. A wave of fractured laughter swept around the group. Everyone knew the price of beating the justice system was high these days, especially for those whose line of work was illegal narcotics.

After the laughter died, they sat quiet. Upstairs the sound of a stereo battered away at the ears of whoever was listening to it. In the backyard someone was working on his machine, the click of the tools an almost religious chant.

Everyone who wore the colors had to be able to tear his Harley's engine down and reassemble it within one hour. It was a necessary skill in order to join the club. A prerequisite to be a part of the inner circle represented by those in the room was even more impressive. You had to have killed at least one man, and be able to prove it. Those that had and could belonged to the Enforcers. They were the strong arm of the club, the protectors of the turf, the ultimate solution to business problems like the one facing them now.

"Gehlen, what have you got?" the Monk reached out his long arm and snatched a filterless Camel from its open pack. Sticking the end with the cigarette's logo between his bearded lips, he lit up and drew the tar-laden smoke deeply into his lungs.

The fourth rider present was called Gehlen at his own request. His position in the club was twofold; he served as their sergeant at arms and intelligence chief. His military occupational specialty in the Navy had brought him into the world of agents and classified operations, although he never did more than general clerical duties. Gehlen had seen himself as part of the dark world of spies and agents, and his fascination for the trade had led him to read countless books on the subject.

Germany's intelligence master, General Reinhard Gehlen, became his role model. After being discharged for coming up positive during a random drug test, he drifted into the L.A. outlaw scene, becoming the Monk's most trusted adviser in the club's hierarchy.

All anyone ever knew him by was the name Gehlen, which he had taken to honor his notorious idol.

The biker spoke, his voice low, purposefully conspiratorial for effect. "My contacts tell me that everything we've heard is true. Dancer is planning to pull the amphetamine business out from under anyone not part of his organization. I also hear he's got support from some of the others along the coast. If he puts in a super-lab, and if he puts it where we think he is . . . then we could be in deep shit."

"So, tell me something I haven't already figured the fuck out, man!" exploded the Monk. The others recoiled at the outburst, their fear of the outlaw president an almost tangible member of the group.

Gehlen continued. "I gotta bitch over in Venice who's a crystal princess. She's been snortin' the shit ever since coming to town to make movies." A burst of guffaws shook the bikers; they'd heard this story before. "Anyway, I introduced her to a guy in the business who makes commercials, and she did a few for him. Shit happens, and now she's hanging around with Mr. Tony Dancer's bodyguard on a regular basis."

Their eyes lit up at the junior spy master's revelation. Eagerly they leaned forward, all except the Monk, who hadn't moved since the meeting began.

"The bitch told me last night that Tony-boy is opening some new vacation dump up on Christmas Eve. He's takin' a few of his people with him, the gunner and this bitch included. She says her asshole boyfriend dropped a dime about her being able to get as much meth as she wants while they're busy partying . . . coke, too."

"She knows where the fucking lab is!" interjected the Monk.

"You got it," answered Gehlen.

The Monk stood. His massive body was the product of both a natural build and hours of pumping weights in prison. Striding over to the bar, where he pulled a cold one from an open cooler on the floor, he turned and spoke. "If Dancer's lab opens we're outta fuckin' business. He'll flood L.A. with cheap speed, and he'll probably snitch off our cookers to the Oregon cops. That happens and we're fucked all the way around."

"So whatta we do?" snorted Roadrash, a puzzled look on his pockmarked face.

"We're gonna hit Dancer and his friggin' lab."

They were all looking at him now. Hit a major player like Dancer? That was serious shit, and they all knew it. They also knew that there would be no way of changing the Monk's mind once he decided on a course of action. They were committed, the only thing left to do was find out who was going, and when.

"Who goes?" ventured Gehlen.

The Monk furrowed his brow as he considered the question.

Not only did his choices have to be reliable as shooters, they had to be politically answerable, too. That meant those who might replace him if things didn't go well, or that could betray him if left behind to their own devices. Looking at Gehlen, he said, "I want you and Bill for sure. Hardpan is pretty handy with a shotgun, so include him. Bill?" The club's VP grunted at the sound of his name. "Bill, you pick two more Enforcers who've done some major jobs. That'll make six of us, plus I want a driver. Maybe one of our associate members from the area?"

Gehlen threw out a name they all agreed on. Then Bill brought up the question of weapons. "What kind of hardware we looking at, Monk?"

"Both the Super 90's, and either the MACs or the Uzis. I'll take my CAR-15 . . . You get a suppressor for it yet?" Bill nodded in the affirmative. "Good. Make sure we've got plenty of magazines for the subs, and double-aught buck for the boomers. If people want to take a pistol, that's cool with me. I want the shit moved north by road no later than the end of this week. Stash everything with the driver. Any questions?"

"Yeah, maybe one?" quipped Roadrash.

The Monk stared hard at the man, and when he answered his voice left no doubt as to his feelings. "You ain't got no questions for me, asshole, cause you ain't along for the ride. So shut the fuck up before I rip your lungs out and clean these dirty-ass windows of ours with 'em!"

The completely cowed biker seemed to shrivel into his chair, his eyes darting around the room, seeking some understanding from his comrades but finding only the amusement of a human wolfpack.

"When does it go down, Monk?"

The huge biker turned to the calendar behind the bar and ran his scarred finger over the month of December. "We hit 'em the night before Christmas, after their little party's over and they're all tucked in, waiting for Santa."

"You want me to put the squeeze on my little girl?" asked Gehlen in a hopeful tone of voice.

The Monk leaned back onto the bar, clamping both his hands over its edge. "You're damned right! You tell Sweetcakes that we want all the info she can pump outta her jerk-off boyfriend. Tell her if she does good you'll get her a role opposite Arnold Schwarzenegger, or some bullshit like that. If she tries to back out, tell her she'll end up doing plastic-surgery commercials with 'before and after' shots. . . ."

Gehlen grinned, his face a torturer's mask. "She'll do her part, Monk. She's hungry, dumb, and hooked." He paused a moment as a thought struck him. "What if she's there when we bust in?"

The Monk sucked the last drops from the bottle, then dropped it to the floor, where it exploded, sending shards of glass shrapnel sliding across the tire-tracked linoleum tiles. "If she's around when we blow their asses off, she gets to eat a faceful of lead just like everyone else. If she makes it back to L.A. then we waste her here. She's a loose end, man, and loose ends always need to be fixed so they don't fuck things up. Right?"

CHAPTER

13

Thornton was downstairs in the living room, checking his own calendar. Christmas Eve was nine days away, and the team's pace was at fever pitch. Bailey had left before dawn for the Air National Guard base in Portland. He would be picking up their weaponry and support equipment, then returning to Cannon Beach. Billings had approved their telefaxed request and ordered everything from stockpiles at Quantico. Beginning that evening the team would be rehearsing the actual assault as well as familiarizing themselves with their gear.

The DEA agent had arranged for them to use a little-known military reservation across the Oregon border in Washington state. They would fly there in the afternoons in one of the DEA's helicopters, returning well before first light to a small LZ they'd selected atop a hill several klicks from their base. A van, carefully hidden off the highway, would serve as their transport back to the house.

Upstairs the men were sleeping. They'd been kept up late while Hartung delivered their warning order. Afterward they had been issued uniforms and combat harnesses. The sergeant major himself had overseen their efforts to set up the harnesses so that each item was exactly where it was supposed to be. If anyone went down the others would be able to retrieve what they might need from him by a tactile recon of the man's equipment. Under the stress of night combat there was no time for dragging out flashlights and searching piecemeal for something like a blasting cap.

No one had been permitted to sleep until they'd passed the sergeant major's inspection.

Uniform-wise, they'd settled on a tiger-stripe pattern like the ones from Vietnam. Silver had found a firm that marketed the uniform in a magazine he'd picked up while shopping for groceries. Cut like the current issue battle fatigues, everyone felt the pattern was the finest available for night operations. Thornton ordered three sets per man. They were already breaking in their issue jungle boots, Hartung ensuring they had the current "Panama" lug pattern rather than the original Vietnam one. Headgear was restricted to headbands made from OD green first-aid cravats. As everyone would be wearing voice-activated radios, hats were impractical.

Thornton closed his eyes and began massaging his temples to ease the tension. Nine days. Billings was now sending them two SITREPs a day from his D.C. office. Everybody was keeping to his part in the scenario, although Dancer was now reported to be leaving L.A. several days ahead of the others. Probably to check things out for himself, thought Thornton. He can't afford any surprises given what he's putting together, so it would make sense that he'd want to arrive at Alpine early. They had managed to keep secret the discovery of East's body. Bailey had mentioned to Thornton that two agents working out of San Diego had uncovered a shipment of cocaine due to be smuggled across the border within the week. Was there a connection between the coke, Dancer, and Alpine?

The Southern California task force was pulling out the stops to find out. In what appeared to be an unrelated matter, someone had shot the shit out of several bikers belonging to the club that provided muscle for Dancer's organization. Bailey had described it as a fairly professional ambush, with no suspects apprehended. "Those motorcycle assholes are always looking to blow each other away," he ruminated as he browsed through the report. "With all the fucking gangbangers running around now, we'll probably never know who pulled the trigger and why." He'd dropped the report into their burn bag for disposal.

Heading for the kitchen, he reminded himself that he had lunch planned with Linda that afternoon. Their relationship was slowly maturing, although he hadn't had much time for her since the team took up residence. He was pleased that she avoided asking too many questions about his "friends" and their sudden arrival. Out of character for an aspiring journalist, he mused. But he appreciated her consideration. It meant he didn't have to lie to her . . . too much. Reaching for the wall phone, he heard the van pulling into the garage, its door activated by Bailey's remote-control device. He decided to postpone calling Linda for the moment, knowing that Calvin would probably want some help getting everything unloaded.

Lee had given them his recommendations based on the intelligence reports provided and the nature of the mission. "The package you want is a combination of heavy firepower, light weight, and extreme reliability," he said. "In addition, we'll be working at night under what is being forecast as favorable weather conditions. If we can get night-vision optics, and I mean the new stuff, we'll be able to engage whatever they've got without tripping over the potted plants."

It had been Bailey who had brought up the subject of laser sights, with Lee in full agreement that not only were such scopes available, but that technology had refined them to the point where they were practical. Five Armatron Night Rangers had been ordered directly from the factory. Lee planned to mount both the Belgian 5.56mm FN Minimis with lasers, as well as Thornton's suppressed Colt 9mm SMG. The remaining scopes would serve as backup units if any of their primaries were damaged during training.

Both Lee and Silver would carry the Army's new squad automatic weapons plus an additional 800 rounds of ammunition apiece. In addition Jason would hump a sawed-off twelve-gauge Remington 870 to open any locked doors.

"The Minimi is hell on wheels, Bo," enthused his light-weapons specialist. "It's belt-fed from a two hundred–round high-impact plastic box, has a manageable rate of fire, is light, easy to operate, and with a laser you'll be able to do all of your firing from the assault position."

"When's the last time you fired one of these hummers?" asked Hartung.

"About three months ago up at Devens. We were doing some testing with a team from the Tenth and had four new SAWs on the line. I burned over two thousand rounds through one gun in about forty-five minutes. No jams, no malfunctions. It's a damn fine weapon, Frank."

"Order three," laughed Hartung, who had cut his teeth on .30-caliber Brownings. "I could use one in my truck. . . ."

Each man had put in his preference for a handgun. Silver opting for a Smith and Wesson 645 with suppressor, Thornton preferring a Belgian-made Hi-Power, and Lee selecting a Glock 17. Hartung suggested they all carry a minimum of three magazines apiece, which was agreed upon. "You want anything, Frank?" asked Bailey as he was jotting down their lethal laundry list.

"Naw, I'll be fine once I'm airborne. Got me one of Mar's big SERE knives while we were getting Bo's rubber stabbers in Lake Oswego. If I need anything more than that, then our shit's weak."

They nodded agreement. The sergeant major's job as covey was to provide an airborne commo link between the team and Bailey's people, who would be several miles away from Alpine when they went in. He would also extract the team once the lab was blown and Dancer and company liquidated. If Frank needed to come in shooting, they were out of luck. Bailey's people were only there to seal the site and clean up the mess afterward. This time there wouldn't be a Spike team to pull their ashes out of the fire.

Thornton himself had inspected each of the knives the men had brought with them. His own Randall had arrived two days after Hartung shipped it, and was in excellent condition, considering how long he'd been carrying it . . . and where. Lee favored a custom blade called The Force from Phill Hartsfield. It had been with him for two years, his previous knife having been "left behind" during a mission along the Nicaraguan border. Silver, who had been the top dog of his recon class in Nha Trang, was partial to the SOG Bowie, like the one given him upon graduation. He had left the original home, electing to purchase a replacement from SOG Specialty Knives. Thornton was impressed with its quality. Each of the commandos' knives was mounted either upside down on the left shoulder strap of their combat harness, or carried on the right side of the pistol belt between two ammo pouches.

He had no doubts that they were once again fully capable and willing to use the weapons if forced to.

Stepping into the garage, Thornton was greeted by a red

dot merrily dancing across his chest. Leaning out of the van's passenger window was Bailey, one of the lasers in his hand. "These are bad, bad, very bad things, my man," he whispered. "If we'd had this shit down south we could have sincerely fucked up Ortega's boys, and I mean with no problem at all!"

"Turn that damn thing off," rumbled Thornton as he stared at the quarter-sized circle. "Makes me nervous just seeing it."

Bailey laughed. "Yeah, well Billings sent three Minimis out. Guess he figured we might need a spare. I got your subgun, and it looks *sweet*! Two suppressors in the box, so don't worry about blowing one out over the next week. We got the new nine-millimeter subsonic shit that the SEALs have been using, and regular stuff for the handguns."

Peering into the back of the van, Thornton asked about Silver's explosives. "No sweat, there," responded Bailey. "The boys at Quantico shipped ten pounds of C-4, time pencils, igniters, and two claymores, like Jason asked for. We also got the stun grenades, several feet of M-460 Thunder Strip, grenade fuses, twenty rounds of Shok Lock for the twelve-gauge, and fifteen Stingballs."

"I still don't know why that sawed-off Ranger wants the damn claymores," grunted Thornton. "But he does, and he's the one carrying the shit."

"Well, demo guys are a little weird. If Silver thinks he might need an antipersonnel mine, that's okay with me. Shit, maybe he's paranoid about covering his back while he's rigging the lab."

"You got that right, Sarge," agreed Thornton. "Let's get this stuff unloaded before we wake 'em up. I want to recheck the lists and eyeball the merchandise before we load out for Camp Sequoia tonight."

"Let's do it," agreed the agent.

Thornton punched the drug buster hard in the shoulder. He hummed Christmas carols as they uncrated the tools of their trade.

CHAPTER

██████████

14

Magnumson raised himself off the bed and stretched. Glancing at his watch, he was reminded that Dancer wanted to do some last-minute shopping before they left L.A. Turning, he allowed himself to savor the naked beauty of the actress he'd been seeing since Tony's last bash. She's definitely a looker, he thought to himself, about the best one I've been with since leaving the Crotch. Too bad she's gonna burn herself out on that shit. Shaking his head, he grabbed a towel from the shelf as he entered the bathroom to shower.

The girl hardly noticed the giant bodyguard leave. She was propped up against the bed's headboard, a mirror the size and shape of a saucer firmly braced between her stupendous breasts. Neatly chopped into several lines was the reward for pleasing Dancer's gunslinger. Cocaine. Ninety-eight percent pure and straight from the fields of Juan Valdez. Coffee wasn't Colombia's only cash crop.

Carefully twisting so she could reach the hand-fashioned silver straw Magnumson had given her, she gently rubbed and cleaned out her nose. Coke was *sooo* much finer than speed, she thought. At least it didn't leave you exhausted and looking like hell once you came down. But expensive! Good God, how much it cost! Unless, of course, you had a connection who could turn you on for free. She giggled at her luck with the former Marine. Now *he* was a connection!

With half an ear she heard the shower being turned on, its hard spray beating a tattoo against the frosted glass of the stall. Returning her attention to the cocaine, she carefully placed one end of the metal straw at the beginning of the first line and began to sniff the white powder into her sinus passages. Almost immediately the powerful drug took hold. Faster now, wanting the hard, pleasurable jolt that only coke gave, she snorted the remaining lines. Her breasts struggled to maintain their hold on the mirror, so powerful were her inhalations. Within seconds she had cleaned her plate. Placing it, along with the straw, on the bedside table, she pulled the silk sheets up around her to wait for Magnumson to return.

When he did he was already half-dressed. "Where ya going, Mag?" Her voice was mistlike, reedy in its tone. Damn, I'm high, she thought.

Magnumson vigorously rubbed his long blond hair with a towel he'd taken from the Beverly Hills Hotel. He tossed it at the golden girl, now sitting up. She allowed the sheet to fall below her waist, noting the rekindled interest in his eyes. "You got time for another one?" she cooed.

Magnumson wished he did. But Dancer had said to pick him up at the house no later than ten-thirty, and he was almost late now. "Naw, babe. Sorry, but I got to get Tony and do some driving. You gonna be here when I get back?" he reached for a sports shirt in the closet, tugging it on, then tucking it into his designer jeans.

"No, honey. I've got a reading up on Sunset after lunch. A walk-on in the new Stallone. I'll probably be there all afternoon, and maybe dinner afterward.

Mag knew. She'd *probably* end up screwing the casting director, or someone who said he was the casting director. This little pillbox should have stayed in Wyoming and married a goat roper. "Yeah, well good luck with it. I'll be with Tony until he cuts me loose. If you don't go out tonight I'll meet you back here. Maybe we can grab a late dinner in Santa Monica?"

She turned to face the mirror behind her, inspecting her looks and thinking about what she would wear to the reading. Maybe the chic high-school cheerleader's ensemble she'd gotten last week? "Yeah, Mag . . . dinner would be great. Let's do it."

The bodyguard grunted at her drug-induced spaciness. He reached under the mattress to retrieve his .380, slipping it into the ankle holster he wore on his right leg. In the car underneath the seat he kept a .380 MAC fully suppressed and loaded. In the glove box were extra magazines for both weapons. In addition to the automatic, he carried a small boot knife he'd picked up at a Value Mart Sporting Goods. It wasn't an expensive piece, but it would do the job and he could leave it without remorse or fear that it could be traced back to him.

Eyeing the girl as she admired herself in the mirror, he wished he had time to jump her again, but Dancer's rules were strict, and he was as subject to them as anyone else.

He was about to leave when her voice curled around him one more time. "When we leaving for Christmas, Mag? I need to do some shopping, and I need an address or a phone number in case I get this part."

Fat chance of that, he thought, smirking. "We'll be haulin' outta here the day after tomorrow. Tell your movie buddies they can leave a message at Tony's office. Don't bring a lot, you can always shop up there."

"Where's 'there,' honey?"

Magnumson sat down on the edge of the bed. "It's a ski resort in Oregon, somewhere near Mount Jefferson. It's got all the latest ski shit you can want, plus more."

"More what?" she asked, leaning forward to allow him a front-row view of her cleavage as it swayed with her movement.

His eyes were glued to her chest. "More stuff to put up your pretty little nose than you can begin to imagine," he croaked. "Tony's got a lab, with some of the best meth makers in the country working for him. If you're good to me I'll show it to you once we've got some time to ourselves."

"I'm *always* good to you, Mag honey . . . and I'd *love* to see this place where they make my favorite flavors." She gently kissed him, then bit into his lower lip just enough to make him wince.

"Yeah, yeah, you got it, hon. You just get yourself ready to go and we'll really party, come Christmas." Magnumson jumped up and headed for the door, his concentration ruined by the girl's massive temptations. Before closing the door, he turned and cautioned her to keep everything he had told her between the two of them. She responded by blowing him a kiss and climbing out of the bed, her fantastic body making him slam the door in retreat.

Instead of showering she went directly to the phone. Pulling her handbag into her lap, she dug through the litter that filled it, finally finding her address book. Opening it, she flipped through the pages until she found Gehlen's name. Repeating the number to herself, she dialed, hoping to catch the creepy biker in so she wouldn't have to call him later. The phone rang several times before it was answered.

"Yeah?"

"Gehlen?"

"Who wants to know?" asked the guarded voice on the other end.

"It's Terri."

The coolness left as Gehlen recognized her. Must be high again, he reflected to himself, she always sounds different when she's straight. "Hey, babe, sorry I didn't recognize you. You're soundin' good."

She rolled her eyes upward. Gehlen was *such* a creep! Why he'd been the first person she'd met after arriving from Lander, she'd never know. All she wanted was a quick bite to eat, and the next thing she knew he was sitting next to her. One thing led to another and she was buying her dope from him. He'd gotten her a connection with some commercial makers, and she'd earned some money and some friends. But he wouldn't go away. Now she was having to supply him with information about Mag's boss, which she knew would make the big oaf mad as hell if he knew.

"I got what you want, Gehlen, so let's cut the bullshit."

"Watch your mouth, babe," he warned. "You piss me off and I'll make sure your jarhead boyfriend learns about your business with me . . . and he'll cut you just as bad as I will, except for one thing."

"What's that . . . ?" she asked, now suddenly frightened.

"I'll let you live afterward."

She swallowed. Not even the coke could keep the fear from her voice as she told the vicious animal at the other end everything Magnumson had confided to her. When she was finished, she stopped speaking, an uncomfortable silence between them.

Finally Gehlen spoke as she was about to hang up. "That all, sweetcheeks?"

"Yeah. I've told you everything. We're supposed to fly up to this resort . . . I think he called it Alpine . . . and we're not coming back until after New Year's."

Gehlen smiled at the news. The Monk would be very happy with him. Now they could move and get things ready for Mr. Dancer's last big bash of the year.

Gehlen was going to make sure that he saw his little Jezebel when they hit Dancer. She was dead meat, now that her usefulness to him was over, plus he didn't like her tone of voice. Being pretty didn't give her the right to talk to him like he was a lump of whale shit. "Okay, Terri, ya done good and we're even. You ain't gonna hear from me no more after this. You be cool and do your thing, nobody's ever gonna know about how you helped me, dig?"

She sighed. "Yeah, Gehlen. Hey, thanks for all your help, man, I mean, you really aren't that bad a guy . . . especially for a biker."

Man, was this chick *dumb,* he thought. He would be doing Hollywood and moviegoers the world over a favor by waxing her. "Hey, you're not bad either . . . for a girl. Take care babe . . . and good luck! Maybe I'll see you in the movies?"

After hanging up, she ran to the bathroom, her throat clogging with a sudden surge of vomit until she reached the sanctuary of the porcelain toilet. The slimy sound of Gehlen's froglike voice ricocheted inside her head, its grossness driving her deeper into the toilet's bowels as she struggled to rid herself of last night's dinner, this morning's indulgence, and the mental picture of herself doing plastic-surgery spots on late-night television.

15

The Monk listened intently to Gehlen. When he'd finished, the proto-Nazi sat back in his chair and lit up a joint. Dragging in a healthy hit of the dank, sweet-smelling smoke, he waited for the chief Enforcer to speak. There were only the two of them present this time, the Monk didn't trust any of the others to give him the kind of advice he needed.

Gehlen was coming on to the smoke when the Monk spoke. His voice was low, the tone reminding Gehlen of one of the big Harleys they rode. "I want Lucas and Double Drop on this one. Pass the word to 'em today."

Gehlen nodded his understanding.

The Monk stood up and lumbered across the room. Staring out onto the street, he coughed, spitting a large brownish green glob of sputum into what served as their front yard. Turning back inside the room, he looked straight at Gehlen, his eyes smoldering with an intense heat that burned somewhere deep inside him. Gehlen dared not move, nor did he speak. The Monk was a fearsome presence when he was like this. The Enforcers called this mood his "killing rage," and Gehlen didn't doubt their assessment a bit.

"You and me are flyin' up there the same evening. Have the driver meet us at whatever hick airport we have to land at. The other two drive. No sense attracting any attention, especially since our fracas with the Free Wheelers." The Monk emitted a low chuckle. "The guns up there yet?"

"Yeah, Monk. We pulled them out right after you talked with us. They're with our connection; I verified that myself."

"Good. Today's the nineteenth . . . right?" Again Gehlen

nodded. "That means asshole is leaving on the twenty-first if your bitch's information is righteous. Looks to me like he plans to get into town early, check out the action, make sure everything's ready for his party, then wait for the others so he can play the perfect host."

Gehlen was definitely high. He thought about what the biker chieftain had said and commented that it seemed to make sense. "So we go up a day after him and check out this resort, like doin' a mini-recon or something, huh?"

The Monk returned to his chair. If he noticed his intelligence lieutenant's lack of concentration he didn't seem to care. "Right on. We get there a couple of days before the hit, check things out while keeping a low profile. Come Christmas Eve, we'll wait until the partying has died down, then sneaky-pete in on 'em and waste whoever we find. We get back on the road that night and head for the Portland chapter's clubhouse. They'll be our alibi if the pigs come askin' questions."

"Sounds good to me, Monk." Gehlen gathered what he could find of his senses and prepared to leave. "I'll get ahold of Lucas and DD, you want me to make the plane reservations, too?" The Monk grunted, indicating to Gehlen that he was to coordinate everyone's travel plans. "Anything else, Monk?" he asked.

The sullen biker stared at the floor, his brows arched in thought. "Yeah, make sure to send the Free Wheelers a nice wreath. No card . . . they'll know who it's from."

CHAPTER
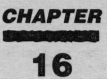
16

"Go! Go! Go!" bellowed Thornton. They careened along a narrow wooded pathway, the tangerine glow of fifty-foot flames casting demonic distortions around their camouflaged figures as they bobbed and weaved over broken ground. A secondary explosion erupted behind them, sending molten metal and splintered wood high into the air. Above the din they could hear the steady whop-whop-whop of the extraction ship as it searched for the clearing that was their pick-up zone.

A cacophony of shots broke out on their left flank, the hornetlike buzz of the rounds breaking over the team's heads as they pushed toward the descending helicopter's dark silhouette. As soon as the point man burst out into the clearing, he dropped to one knee, the others doing the same as they watched him through their XM-500 nightvision goggles. Huskily gulping huge draughts of oxygen, they quickly adjusted themselves so they formed a defensive triangle.

"Guns up!" screamed Silver as both Thornton and Lee brought their weapons to bear on the surrounding darkness. There was no sign of pursuit. "Stand by for extraction!" Hartung's energy-soaked voice snapped through their earphones as the UH-1H began to sink toward the PZ's grass-covered scalp.

Thornton chanced a quick look upward at an all-too-familiar sight. Leaning out over the skids were both Hartung and the Huey's crew chief. Their goggle-shrouded eyes searched the ground below for obstacles, their lips in constant motion as they guided the pilot in. The ship itself was as black as Satan's teeth. No lights were visible, only the dull red blush of the instrument panel illuminated the figures of the flight crew in their plexiglass cocoon. Thornton's attention returned to the bush, a rapid check ensuring that the others were doing the same.

As the slick reached a hover point only inches from the ground, Hartung bellowed, "Load!" Lee resumed point, leading in a fast rush toward the Huey's doorless opening. Thornton followed the running man, swinging his head from side to side as he maintained a close watch along their route, he spun around to check their rear, his Minimi's barrel tracing a deadly arc while the button-activated laser played hide and seek among the trees. If they were pursued, Silver would grind the hunters into bloody mush with long, ripping bursts from the SAW.

Hartung spoke into his mike, its cable connected to the ship's internal net so that members of the crew could communicate between themselves. "Here they come, Chief. Stand by to receive visitors on the portside!" Snuggled up between the pilot and copilot's seats, the chief nodded his acknowledgment. He turned and patted his commander deftly on the shoulder, letting him know they were nearly ready to get the hell off the deck. Both pilots could see knifelike fingers of fire ripping apart the curtain of night. They waited patiently, old hands at their jobs and no strangers to midnight riders.

Lee exploded through the slick's open doorway with the intensity of the Boz crunching Denver's offensive line. He had begun his leap three feet from the hovering ship. Mustering every ounce of adrenaline left in him, he had thrown himself aboard, narrowly missing Hartung, standing atop the skid. Balling himself up as soon as he struck the aluminum floor plates, he bounced against the fire wall before coming to a stop. Behind him came Thornton, whose cheek glanced off the heels of Lee's snow-soaked jungle boots. He, too, rolled himself into a protective ball, his back facing the door as Silver's figure loomed into view.

Moving at a steady pace, the team's tail gunner checked his position with a backward glance every other step, his weapon remaining at the ready should the unarmed ship begin taking rounds from the flickering tree line. When the former LRRP was within arm's reach, Hartung clamped a gloved hand over his shoulder and pulled him up over the skid and onto the deck. As soon as the gunner was secured, Hartung launched himself into the "hellhole," gesturing at the crew chief that they could leave.

With a rush of turbine-generated power, the Huey dashed forward toward the treetops. Gently massaging his stick, the pilot goosed them over shaggy boughs, although Silver would later swear he had felt branches slapping at his dangling feet as they cleared the PZ. The chopper dropped over a ridgeline and began its circuitous journey back to the coast.

Inside, the men began checking equipment. Thornton watched each man's expression as the helicopter contoured the earth's face, sometimes barely fifty feet above the ground. He didn't see any unnatural stress on either Lee's or Silver's features. Their actions were fluid, controlled, each exhibiting a purpose, as they slipped their weapons on "safe" before conducting a tactile inventory of their harness items.

Bracing himself against the bird's fire wall, Thornton reviewed the night's training exercise. It was their fifth full dress rehearsal and he was almost satisfied with the team's performance. With barely seventy-two hours left before the real thing, he had to push them toward perfection. He and Frank were thinking of conducting at least two more runs the following evening.

In his heart he knew they were already damned good. Good enough to probably pull it off tonight. But "probably" wasn't acceptable. Thornton remembered the ramrod-straight special-warfare instructor at Bragg who had been his TAC during phase one.

The man had served under Aaron Bank when that OSS veteran activated the 10th Special Forces Group in the early fifties. His wisdom had been earned the hard way, and his determination to pass it on to only the most deserving caused many of Thornton's classmates to fall by the wayside. Standing on the instructor's platform, he preached the "six-P theory" to them. "Gentlemen," he advised, "if you want to live longer than a sperm cell on a toilet seat, you'd better practice the following principle: Prior planning prevents piss-poor performance." Thornton had listened well, and he'd stayed alive while others died foolishly.

The chopper slipped left and headed out toward the Port of Portland. The pilot turned on their navigation lights so that they were now part of the night's normal air-traffic flow. Hartung handed out headsets so that the men could talk to each other, his humped form sidestepping around the team in the cramped confines of the Huey.

Three days earlier, he and the crew chief had stripped the interior furnishings from the ship normally reserved for touring DEA officials. The pilots had been brought in from SOCOM's new Special Operations wing in Florida, and Thornton had to admit they were number one in every respect. It was at Frank's insistence that the doors were removed, as well as the OD paint job. "No doors and no recognizable coloring, damn it!" he raged over the phone. This ain't no embassy run we're planning . . . so you can just get that bird prepped the way I've told you or you can go in yourself!"

As usual the sergeant major got his way.

Frank's voice boomed into his headset as they once again veered left and began the flight along the picturesque Oregon coastline. A half-moon illuminated their way through the chilly December skies, reminding Thornton of how happy he was to be wearing his long underwear. Even so, it was cold as hell with both doorways vacant. "How'd it go, stud?" quizzed Hartung.

"We looked good, Frank." With the roar of the rotors above them and the wind whipping inside the ship, Thornton was forced to shout into the tiny mike. "There was a problem with one of the lasers slipping off its mount on Silver's Minimi. But some Lok-Tite should cure that ASAP." Huddled next to the crew chief, Hartung nodded. "Jason and I have got door-busting down pat, and Lee tosses Stingballs like a major-league pitcher! I figure a coupla more practice runs and we'll be ready to kick ass and take names."

The team settled in for the remainder of the flight. Bunching up close, they shared their body heat, making the trip bearable. Everyone but the aircrew dropped into a half-slumber, seeking what rest was possible until they landed. Even then they would spend several hours cleaning and inspecting their equipment before being allowed to sleep. No one expected any slack, regardless of how late they got back or how tired they were. You took care of your equipment so it would take care of you.

The crew chief began shaking them awake when they were five minutes out from the hilltop. Outside, the sun was beginning to rise, the first hints of false dawn tinting the horizon. Moments later their LZ came into view. Below it, they could see the road where Bailey waited with the van. Stretching as best they could, the team shook itself into action. Removing their goggles and stuffing them into a kit bag, the men adjusted the headpieces of their Motorola radios, testing their internal commo net by greeting each other with casual good-mornings.

The radios were Silver's solution to the problem of communicating quickly and quietly during both movement on the ground or in a firefight. The units were no larger than the average Sony Walkman, and utilized a single-looped earphone with voice-activated boom mikes. By securing the headset beneath their cravats, then taping the transmitter-receiver to the right shoulder strap of their combat harnesses, the team was able to maintain voice communications. Both Hartung and Bailey had their own units so they could monitor the team's activities and respond to any emergency situation that might arise.

"You awake back there, Sergeant Major?" asked the pilot, who had learned his trade with the 101st in Vietnam.

"Roger that, sir," responded Hartung, cinching the bag full of goggles shut.

"We're about to drop you off in about one mike. The AO looks clear, we spotted your transport as we were coming in. How copy?"

"Good copy, *Dai Uy*. Thanks for the lift; that was a damn fine piece of flying you boys did for us!"

"We thank you kindly for the compliment," noted the pilot, a hint of pride in his voice. "Same time, same place tonight?" he asked.

"That's affirmative," acknowledged Hartung. After trading hand signals with the crew chief, Hartung, veteran of more covey flights than he cared to remember, stripped off the chopper's headphones and motioned for the others to do the same. The bird suddenly dropped toward the tiny LZ, stopping several feet above its sandy surface. At the crew chief's command, they jumped as one from the slick, landing stiffly before running toward the concealment of the tree line. Setting up a perimeter with one man at each of the cardinal directions, they waited until the Huey was out of earshot before forming up and moving down the rough dirt trail that would take them to the highway.

With Lee on point maintaining noise discipline and moving so they were each roughly five meters apart, the team ground out a steady pace. Reaching a bend in the trail that overlooked the highway, they stopped. Thornton moved up to where Lee was kneeling and spoke briskly into his mike. Several seconds passed before Bailey responded.

"Hey, good buddy, you boys ready to go home?"

"You got that right, my man. You still parked by the diner?"

"A-firma-teevo! Bring 'em on in, there's hot chow a-wait-in'!"

Thornton heard the men chuckle softly behind him, and couldn't help but crack a smile himself. With so many CB outfits around, it made sense to blend their communications in with normal radio banter on the off-chance that someone might monitor their transmissions. It was bad enough having the chopper come in as it had to, although anyone interested would think it was one of the many Forest Service birds that patrolled the beaches and hillsides on a daily basis.

Hearing the van's engine start, Thornton nodded for Lee to take them down to where Bailey would meet them. Five minutes later they were safely hidden away behind the reflective windows installed for just that purpose, and were on their way back to Cannon Beach and the FOB.

After finishing the hearty breakfast Bailey had prepared before picking them up, the men gathered their weapons and moved out into the living room. They began inspecting their gear for damage as Hartung brought out two steaming pots of strong black coffee. Its heady aroma filled the room, causing the men to nod in appreciation as they grabbed their cups and filled up. Watching them chatting and joking with each other, Bailey turned to Hartung. "You'll make somebody a fine little wife one day, Sergeant Major."

"Fuck you and the horse you rode in on, squid-lips," came the reply. Both men elbowed each other in mock combat.

"How they lookin'?" asked Bailey, suddenly serious.

"Damn good from what I see. Bo thinks they're ready, although I know he'd like to have more time."

Bailey grunted his concurrence. "Time is what we're about out of, Frank. I talked with Bo while everyone was eating. Dancer is en route from L.A. this morning. Billings wants us ready to move to the MSS—mission support site—the day after tomorrow. I've got our latest intelligence report on Alpine ready to brief, and I think we'd better plan on doing it before everyone sacks out."

"What's Bo say?" asked Hartung. But before Bailey could reply, Thornton strolled into the living room and asked for everyone's attention.

"Okay, let's listen up!" commanded Thornton. The men ceased chattering and stopped whatever it was they were doing as soon as they heard the tone in their team leader's voice. As soon as he had their undivided attention, Thornton continued.

"Get comfortable, gentlemen, we got some talkin' to do before anyone can plan on getting any rack time." Each man sought out a comfortable chair or place on the floor, taking his weapon with him for something to work on as the meeting progressed. Thornton was impressed by their lack of grumbling or complaints.

Once they were settled, he began speaking. For nearly thirty minutes they discussed the last several days of training, up to and including the previous evening's exercise. Each man gave his opinions and observations concerning every facet of the planned assault, good points and bad. When they were finished, Thornton offered his own assessment of their progress, then asked Bailey to step forward. All eyes turned to the DEA agent, whom they'd come to know and trust. He was one of them and he felt their comradeship as he took the floor from Thornton.

"Everyone's concerns have been noted, and we'll see what we can do about them ASAP. Frank can get up with the chopper crew this afternoon and see about repadding the bird, and I agree that we should carry the extra SAW onboard just in case we might need it. In the meantime it appears that we'll be leaving somewhat sooner than originally planned." They looked up with great interest.

"What's the scoop, Cal?" It was Silver, busily inspecting his demo bag's contents while he spoke.

"Intel has the primary target leaving Southern California this morning. Traveling with him is his security thug and a coupla party girls. San Diego DEA reports that a shipment of two hundred twenty-five keys crossed the border last night and headed for Los Angeles. One of their agents is part of the escort team. He reported they broke the shipment up into two parts once it hit L.A. What's of interest is that one hundred twenty-five keys got salted away in a safe house owned by Dancer, the other hundred keys went to the airport and into the man's personal Lear."

"Looks like our man plans on making everyone's Christmas a merry one," Lee snorted.

"That or he's piggy-backed his own private deal at the expense of his business partners. Remember, Sweet Tony controls most of the Valley's flow of precious powders. There are other players out for a piece of that pie, and if they can provide quality product at less cost to the consumer . . ."

"*They* get to run the roost!" finished Hartung.

"Exactly."

It was Thornton's turn to comment. He sat at the coffee table, his Colt subgun broken down, a cleaning rod sticking out of the barrel. "So we can plan on finding not only a major stockpile of methamphetamine, but about a hundred bricks of coke, too."

"Right." Bailey paused, then broke the news. "We've talked about what goes into setting up a lab like the one we're going to hit. Without going into the chemistry of it, we know there's enough P_2P plus other assorted bullshit chemicals stockpiled at Alpine to blow the lab to hell without any help from a coupla pounds of C-4."

"Which means . . . ?" asked Lee.

"Which means that once Jason sets his charges, you've got precious little time to get out of Dodge. Once the lab goes it's going to look like Dante's Inferno anywhere within three hundred meters of the complex. If you're still within that range, you better dig in . . . and I mean deep!"

The men exchanged glances as they digested the narc's assessment. None of them had ever been inside a speed lab, although Bailey had presented a comprehensive slide and video show to them during their first week at the FOB.

"How do we confirm the primary and his playmates getting toasted?" asked Silver.

This time Hartung spoke, it being his portion of the operation to determine the most suitable way of hitting Dancer. "The team isn't large enough to take out the lab and track down targets at the same time. So we're going to use the lab to whack the bad guys."

"What if they've got a way out?" asked Thornton.

"That would have to be by foot, which isn't likely once any shooting starts, or by chopper which they have two of. The birds are Bell Air Stars, capable of taking five passengers plus the pilot. They're located roughly seven hundred meters from the building . . . which just happens to have a rooftop pad on it. They *could* have an evac plan."

"I can wire the Bells with a half-pound of plastique apiece, and use a command detonation system to blow them if it becomes necessary," ventured Silver.

"We'd have to do it before we hit the lab, but we're planning on going in that way, anyhow." Thornton turned to Silver. "How will you rig the lab if you use the command systems for the birds?"

"Time pencils. Three-minute delay once I bust 'em."

"Okay, let's plan on that." Thornton spread a hand-drawn diagram out on the floor, inviting everyone to gather in close as he illustrated their assault plan with his index finger.

"Bailey's people will be standing by just outside the resort. It's their job to shut down any traffic coming or going once the fireworks start. Frank will be airborne five minutes before we begin our assault. Once he hears us open up, he'll move the bird in so he can extract us within two minutes of getting our call.

"We'll be dropped off by vehicle about three hundred meters west of the heliport. Remember, the complex is separated from the rest of the resort by about a hundred meters. It's surrounded by a security fence. There appears to be nearly two hundred fifty meters of trees, shrubs, and other assorted tourist bullshit between the fence and the condos. We'll be entering through a small service gate past where they keep the choppers. So Silver will have a chance to do his thing before we actually enter the grounds."

"You still want the power blown?" asked the demolitions expert.

"Absolutely. Have you got enough C-4 left after last night and with the additional targets?"

"I could use a few more pounds..." Silver replied. His request brought on a series of hoots and hollers from the team, everyone knowing that demo men *always* seemed to need "just a few more pounds" of whatever it was they were working with.

"Tell Cal how much, and he can get it from the local military. That right, squid?"

"No sweat. We'll just say it's for a DEA training exercise. Happens all the time."

They spent the next two hours reviewing every alternative and contingency the team could think of. By the time Thornton called it quits it was nearly noon. "That's it, everyone grab your gear and get some rest."

"What time you want us up, Bo?" asked Lee as he shouldered his harness.

Thornton looked around at his team. He realized their exhaustion as they stood there before him, weapons and gear hanging from their soiled bodies. The last three weeks had taken their toll. Unless he eased up they could lose the razor-like edge he was attempting to hone. Walking up to Lee, the Special Forces sniper, he slapped him lightly on the back and squeezed his grimy neck. "We'll wake you at twenty-one hundred hours if you're not up before that."

Turning to Hartung, he winked. "Frank, make some late dinner reservations downtown for us. It just occurred to me we'll be working on Christmas Eve, so we'd better plan on having our own celebration before then."

The sergeant major's face lit up in approval. "You got it, Bo. I'll let the pilots know they can sack out after we've rigged the bird this afternoon. Anything else?"

Thornton looked at Bailey. "Dinner okay with you, Cal?"

"If you feel we can pull it together with what we've got, then I've got no objections, Bo."

"Then dinner's at twenty-one thirty, gentlemen. Dress blues and tennis shoes, attendance mandatory. Any questions?"

There were none. With a whoop the men clambered up the stairs, their laughter and joking spilling back down to where Hartung was standing with Bailey. "He's a hell of a One-Zero, isn't he?" marveled Bailey.

Hartung clapped the young narc on the back as they walked out the door and toward the van. "That he is, Calvin, that he damn is. But then that's why your people hired him."

"Airborne and amen!" snorted Bailey.

Hartung shook his head as they backed down the driveway. "Not only do I have to work with a salt-suckin' SEAL, but I gotta listen to him steal my own lines!" he complained.

Upstairs the team was already fast asleep.

CHAPTER

17

The private jet began its final approach, the pilot carefully lining up the sleek nose of the aircraft against the length of runway laid out before him. In the passenger compartment they were peering through the circular windows, pointing and commenting on the crystal clearness of the air and the purity of the snow that covered the ground.

Waiting patiently while the plane taxied towards the terminal were two silver Cadillac limousines. As the plane drew closer, the automobiles' occupants were routed from the comfort of the luxurious land cruisers, and ordered to stand on the snowy tarmac. Their leader was a man of medium height whose face was the definition of ordinary. His only item of distinction was a small gold-plated emblem affixed to the front of his black skullcap. The Trident signified that at one time he had been a member of the Navy's elite SEAL teams.

Stennmaker kept his eyes riveted on the Lear as it plowed through the morning's early snowfall. His team had been waiting for nearly an hour, their time occupied by playing cards and listening to the limos' expensive stereo systems. Out of the Navy for just three years, the SEAL-turned-outlaw had been termed "flaky" by the CIA after submitting an application to the agency's paramilitary section. Stung by their rejection, Stennmaker executed a hard about-face and marched headlong into the turbid world of the hired gun. Not particulary interested in actual *combat* work, he instead made contact with those whose line of business centered around lawyers, guns and money. After a year of freelancing he sold his talents as an instructor to a mercenary training school in Louisiana. It was there that he was introduced to the pro-racist White Ring, and soon afterwards he moved into their Idaho headquarters to become the organization's chief paramilitary instructor.

When "Barf Bag" Suddath had called from Denver asking for a clean team of gunslingers, he'd immediately been interested. Not caring about politics, he was finding the Ring's commando games boring, and their women were uglier than a Kevlar helmet full of hickory-smoked assholes. He'd contracted himself out to the Barf Bag, using his position with the Ring to secure a team of shooters that would do the job. When the call had come to deploy he'd been ready, although he'd had to negotiate a finder's fee with the nazi lovers before he'd been free to leave.

The turbines spun themselves to a stop, allowing the cabin attendant to release the door and drop the stairway for the passengers' departure. Stennmaker gestured two of his men forward to assist them, he himself waiting until he recognized Magnumson leaving the plane. The two men shook hands warmly while exchanging greetings.

"How was the flight?" asked the former SEAL.

"Super! We made good time even though LAX kept us on the ground an extra half hour while some dipshit airlines pilot made an emergency landing." Magnumson turned towards the limos, checking out the men who waited nearby. "They look pretty good, you pick 'em?" he asked.

"Each and every swinging dick. Most are former military or security types. I stayed away from busted-out cops. No need tempting fate."

Nodding his head in sage appreciation the blond gunner spit hard into the snow at his feet. "We got luggage and a shipment in the cargo hold. The blue leather bags are to go directly into the vault at the lab. Mr. Dancer's and my gear go to the penthouse, the girls have their own room on the second floor."

Stennmaker grunted. His men were already loading the plane's payload into the limos and he noticed for the first time the two women Magnumson had referred to. They were definitely lookers, and he couldn't help but admire the way their obviously expensive fur coats wrapped themselves around the women. "Where's the man?" he inquired.

"Still inside. He wants to check some details with us, and lay out the next few days' activities. Any problems I should know about before we see him?"

"Nope. We're one hundred percent secure on site. The boys in the lab are cooking their little brains out to make deadline. No one's as much as looked in our direction since being told they'd have Christmas Eve off. Should be a nice party once the others get here tomorrow."

Magnumson dropped a heavy arm over Stennmaker's shoulders. "Let's go see the man then. I'm sure he's anxious to hear your report." Together they climbed into the richly decorated interior of Dancer's personal jet while outside the ladies received a steady stream of compliments from Stennmaker's now wide awake gun crew.

The joking and light conversation during the drive to Alpine abruptly ceased as the cars drove through the gate leading onto the grounds of the luxury resort. Lining the winding drive like soldiers in winter camouflage stood twin rows of thick tall pine trees, their boughs laden with snowflakes that sparkled in the sunlight. On either side of the trees they could see low-slung cabins with fenced backyards and private entrances. Progressing at a leisurely fifteen miles per hour they crossed a covered wooden bridge that appeared as if it had been lifted out of a picture postcard. Below the bridge ran a wide but shallow stream, its surface now frozen with a thin layer of early winter ice. To their left stood the Manor Lodge. Two stories high with French roofs and stained-glass windows, it housed a restaurant, ski shop, an upstairs and downstairs bar, and a fully equipped exercise facility. Just across the street was a nightclub modeled after the Malamute Saloon in Fairbanks, Alaska. Complete with double swinging doors, a hewn-oak floor, and tin-panny piano, the club was expected to become a favorite with the ski crowd.

"Tony, this place is simply awesome. I had no idea it was this large!" marveled Dancer's guest for the week. She was the executive receptionist for one of the top box-office draws in Hollywood and had met the always-social drug lord at a party given to benefit the city of Burbank's halfway-house program.

"You haven't seen the best of it yet, angel," responded Dancer. "Wait until we come around the bend up here. That's when you'll see what Alpine is all about."

The lead car slowed to negotiate the ice-crusted turn in the road, its heavy tires grinding the fluffy drifts of snow into a mash of muddy slush. Dancer's vehicle followed in the path left by the point team as they suddenly broke into an open expanse of ground that surrounded a fenced stand of pine and fir. On either side of the forested island they could see the magnificent Cascade Mountains, their jagged peaks thrusting into the cold aqua blue of Oregon's winter sky. Silence once again overcame them as they compared the rustic splendor of Alpine to the smog-streaked starkness of downtown Los Angeles.

Traveling in the lead car was Stennmaker, who casually pushed a button on the caddy's dash activating the double front gates that led into the executive lair. The wrought-iron gates rolled quietly back on solid graphite wheels, allowing the limousines to pass between electronic sensors. Speaking quickly into his portable transmitter, Stennmaker alerted the outer perimeter of guards that they were en route and to prepare to offload both guests and luggage. He then secured the gates by once again thumping the hidden switch.

Dancer's Alpine was indeed magnificent.

The length of four family homes and three stories high, the building was constructed from logs and timbers cut in Canada and trucked to the United States. Each piece had been custom trimmed and fit into place by local craftsmen, their talent evident by the way the lodge maintained its interior heat using a massive stone fireplace. A set of hardwood stairs opened onto the eighteen-foot-wide veranda that ran the length of the building. Two more sets of stairs were present at either end. A Grand Entrance doorway constructed from twin pieces of solid oak invited the visitors inside. Before entering they turned to admire the carefully landscaped grounds that intentionally formed a natural buffer between the Cyclone fencing on the outer perimeter and the nucleus of Dancer's retreat.

"Should you care to stroll the grounds go ahead," Dancer informed his rapt guests as they gathered on the porch. "Please use the sidewalks which, by the way, are swept every three hours. You'll notice the miniature lighting system along the walkway. It will allow you to find your way back home at night. Now please, shall we go inside?"

Ordering Stennmaker's men to take the luggage to their rooms, Dancer's headhunter then detailed one man to ensure that the cocaine was installed in the laboratory's vault. Magnumson rejoined the party just as their host was preparing to take everyone on a guided tour. For the next forty-five minutes they were ushered through the downstairs pool and recreation area, then up to the second floor where the majority of the guests would be staying. It was here that Dancer unveiled his personal library, a room with floor-to-ceiling shelves that were interspaced with recognized works of Western art. Ending up in the penthouse suite, Dancer invited them to brunch on a wide assortment of foods prepared in the manor's kitchen. Dancer's own quarters ran the length and width of the structure, with a high-beamed ceiling that was studded with various cut-glass skylights. At the north end of the main room there was a broad sundeck that could be accessed through a sliding glass door. Unique to its construction was the fact that there was no guard railing around the deck's sides, though it was laid with thick outdoor carpet, fully lighted, and clearly meant for outdoor activities.

Only Dancer, Magnumson and Stennmaker knew that the real purpose of the sundeck was to act as an emergency helicopter pad should a rapid departure be necessary.

Finishing their lunch, Dancer passed out room keys and reminded everyone that the majority of the week's guests would be arriving the next day. He then cautioned them as they were leaving to explore their newly discovered surroundings.

"My friends, please feel free to use whatever is provided. My house is your house, and we are preparing to celebrate our Lord's birthday. Remember that as of noon Christmas Eve, those of us here will be the only inhabitants of Alpine Manor. We open officially to the public on New Year's Day." A round of polite applause followed this announcement.

"Is there anything we *shouldn't* do?" asked Magnumson's pie-eyed girlfriend, her question sparking a barrage of laughter from the small group.

"Yes. Actually I had overlooked one thing," replied Dancer. "You mustn't attempt to leave the grounds by any other exit than the front gate. We do have a small portal out back, but it leads to where I keep my helicopters and I believe our power station is back there too. This area is patrolled, for obvious reasons, by Mr. Stennmaker's most capable *and* armed security personnel. For my peace of mind if nothing else, please consider that particular area off limits."

Everyone nodded their understanding. "Are there wolves up here?" The question came from Dancer's holiday companion, a look of mock terror on her face.

"Not as many outside the fence as inside," quipped Magnumson as he tweaked Terri's sumptuous bottom. The group convulsed in laughter at the gunslinger's unusual display of wit.

Dancer clapped his hands together twice, dismissing them. Motioning for Magnumson to stay behind, he walked to one of the massive Pozzi windows that overlooked his wooded domain. "I am pleased with yours and Stennmaker's security preparations." As he spoke he watched a large grey squirrel scampering among the trees, stopping only to nibble at bits and pieces of vegetation still green despite winter's approach. "But I want to go over them again. With all the enemies I have, on both sides of the legal fence, it is possible that someone has heard something about either our meeting or the product. Agreed?"

Magnumson looked directly into the inquiring eyes of his employer. He wondered if Dancer ever really relaxed, knowing that he could not if he wanted to maintain his position as the cartel's kingpin. Indicating with a downward glance at his breast pocket that he wished to smoke, he received a casual hand's wave from Dancer and proceeded to light up. Only after exhaling a long rush of bluish smoke from his lungs did he begin to outline the security measures now in force.

"We have a twelve-man team currently under roof. Two shifts of twelve hours make up the daily rotation. The transformer and choppers got two men on 'em. That's a roving post. The lab is a one-man position located outside the main door in the basement. There's another roving patrol on the grounds, leaving one man here in the building to cover anyone needing backup.

"Firepower wise they're armed with shotguns and pistols, although I've put a submachine gun in with the guy on lab duty. The guns have folding stocks so our people can carry them underneath their coats on an assault sling. Less conspicuous that way."

Dancer signaled his approval. "Where do the guards stay?" he asked.

Taking a liberal swig from an open beer on the table, the head shooter continued. "Their living quarters are located in a building next to the heliport. That way they're out of sight and out of mind during the regular season. For this gig I figured it'd be okay if we put 'em up in the empty rooms on the second floor."

"I like that, Mag. We'll have the major West Coast powers here, and although they'll be bringing in their own protection, it'll be better all the way around if we have everyone under one roof."

Magnumson nodded his head in agreement. "What's the story with the shipments?" he asked.

Dancer moved away from the window and settled himself in an overstuffed chair next to a wood stove that was burning merrily. "Pour me a snifter, please," he ordered. After Magnumson had handed the thick amber liquid to him, he tasted it and continued.

"The coke we'll wrap in fancy paper and hand out to the boys as Christmas gifts. That ought to brighten them up and it'll smooth the way for further transactions. The 'meth' must be finished and broken down no later than Christmas morning. We'll begin moving it that afternoon using Tom's truck network. Already we've received quite a bit of interest from our street distributors. They're excited about the lower price but greater quality."

"Any heat felt from the DEA thing?"

Dancer watched Magnumson carefully before answering. He knew that the man was worried about being connected to the killing of a federal officer, especially a narc. Hell, the damned United States Congress had passed legislation allowing the death penalty for shit like that! It wouldn't affect a man in Dancer's position, but a hired thug like Magnumson was sure to face the chair or needle should a jury of his peers vote him thumbs down. "Nothing. I have heard nothing concerning Agent East since we last chatted. That in itself is somewhat puzzling, as our sources normally would have picked up *something* from the police grapevine. But I wouldn't worry about it. You disposed of him exactly as I told you to, correct?"

Magnumson snubbed out the cigarette, the ember beginning to burn its way into the filter. "Yeah, I did it all like you said, Tony. It's just that hittin' a narc isn't exactly an everyday affair for me, dig?"

Dancer stood and approached his top gun. Putting both arms around him he gave the man a powerful embrace, then gently shook him as a father will his son after a heart-to-heart talk. "Hey! You've been with me for awhile now, eh? Have I ever left you out on the wire by yourself? Ever?" Magnumson shook his head. "If the DEA wants Mr. East, they'll have to find him. In the meantime it's Christmas and we have guests to entertain. The blond bimbo, she's good?"

"Oh yeah, Tony, she's a fine pastime." The reminder of Terri's unbridled ferocity in bed seemed to snap the depression that had come over the executioner. "She's a pistol, but damn does she suck up the dope!"

Dancer released his chaindog, turning back towards the stove and his favorite chair. "Yes, well I want you to enjoy your little friend because after this trip she's not to be associated with either myself or you."

Magnumson waited half a heartbeat before asking his question. "Why's that, Tony?"

"A very reliable source close to the motorcycle crowd told me she was on speaking terms with one of the Speed Kings. Naturally that in itself doesn't mean a whole lot. But given our own business dealings with the Free Wheelers and their recent 'encounter' with what was probably a rival gang, it would be best if Miss Hotpants went back to making pantyhose commercials . . . without your help."

Magnumson growled in disgust. "No sweat, Tony. I'm gettin' a little tired of wondering whose pincushion she's been before I get home anyway. We hit L.A. and she's history, just like you want."

Dancer lifted the now empty brandy glass towards Magnumson in acknowledgment of the man's promise. "Please pour me another, would you Mag? And one for yourself, you've earned it."

Twenty-five miles away, one slightly airsick biker and his huge, perfectly airworthy companion stepped off of the commercial airliner that had just arrived from the City of Angels. They were met by a man whose shoulder-length red hair was tied in a ponytail, and who hurried the pair into his waiting van. Inside the terminal those unfortunate travelers who had sat next to the two outlaws were threatening to have their clothes burned once they reached their prospective hotels. How was it possible that two human beings could be so obnoxious and smell so bad at the same time?

Inside the rapidly moving van The Monk deftly inserted a 30-round magazine of 5.56 calcium dissolvers into his CAR-15, then screwed on its foot-long suppressor. Both of his companions could swear they heard the Maximum Enforcer quietly humming Christmas carols as he prepared himself for battle.

CHAPTER

18

Billings was in conference with two of the junior agents who made up the Alpine strike force. Dressed in street clothes, carrying micro Uzis underneath their down vests, they busily jotted down his instructions, their eyes darting toward the head narc, then back to their notebooks every time he made a point.

Beyond the command tent's flaps lay the hastily erected DEA mission support site. Army GP-Medium tents housed the group of agents and support personnel brought in from field stations around the United States. Three tractor-trailers formed a communications and logistics center, its perimeter marked with a single strand of red engineer's tape. Sequestered to one side was a hastily bulldozed parking lot, its cramped space filled with both official and civilian vehicles. As most of the cars had weapons and munitions locked inside, two armed guards patrolled its borders. Deep within a little-known Army test facility, the MSS was thirty minutes from Alpine Manor by automobile, ten by air. The civilian guard service which normally provided the reservation's security officers had been ordered to pull its people off for several days. In their place Billings installed six DELTA teams to man the single highway entrance to the site and to patrol the immediate area surrounding the buildup of narcotics agents.

Billings's own quarters were situated on the far western side of the MSS. His tent, a GP-Large, would serve as staging area for Thornton's team once they arrived. Instead of engineer's tape, Billings had ordered a fence of triple-roll concertina wire erected around the tent. Two DELTA operatives

manned the entrance, with specific orders as to the credentials
necessary for admittance. Deadly force was authorized.
Shielded by the tent was a single-ship LZ. It was here that
Thornton's team would base, both before and after the assault
against Alpine. Access to the team was limited to Billings,
Bailey, and the flight crew.

Answering final questions from the two agents in front of
him, Billings wished them luck and waited until they'd left the
tent before he began his next task. Standing, he rubbed the
back of his neck with both hands and mentally began checking
off the laundry list of things he had yet to do. At that moment
one of the DELTA people poked his head through the tent
flaps. "Mr. Billings? We've got a chopper en route. Sounds
like he's three or four minutes out."

Billings acknowledged the man with a wave of his hand
and a quick smile. He was impressed with the professionalism
of the SOCOM people. They did their jobs well, asking few
questions and reporting everything.

Grabbing his Alessi shoulder holster, he fitted himself into
its soft harness, then double-checked the Detonics .45 it carried. In addition to the magazine in the weapon, Billings carried two extras. Each was loaded with Remington Silver Tips
and standard-issue government ball ammunition staggered for
the maximum in man-stopping power from the .45 compact.
Along with the Detonics, he carried an AMK Executive folder
on his pants belt, just in case something came along that
needed cutting.

The mechanical drone of the slick was clearly audible now.
All around the camp, eyes began turning upward as the coal
black Huey emerged from the early evening's light. An agent,
busily oiling his Colt Commando, nudged the man next to
him. "Looks like the heavies are here. I wonder who the hell
those guys are?"

His companion briefly scanned the sky as the chopper's
rotor wash began throwing up a snowstorm that successfully
obscured those on board from view. "Man, there ain't nobody
in on this operation who isn't a heavy. You seen any of our
nationally known pencil pushers hanging around?"

The first narc shook his head as he ran through a quick
function check of his weapon.

"That's because we're in on something so hush-hush the management types are persona non grata." The bearded narcotics officer rose and worked the action on his own Benelli Super 90 riot gun. Satisfied with its performance, he continued. "Either that or the boys in fancy pants *don't want* to be anywhere near what might turn into a political nightmare serious enough to flush their years of handjobbing down the drain."

The first agent began loading his magazines, quickly slipping hollow-point rounds underneath the retaining lip with a casualness that betrayed his expertise with the weapon. "You think the dudes in that bird are ours?" he asked.

The shotgunner laughed. "No way, my man, no mutherfuckin' way. Whoever those people are, they have to be the baddest of the bad, and that means independents. We're the good guys, remember? Good guys play by the rules . . . and black choppers with faceless men are definitely non-regulation."

Inside the descending aircraft, Thornton tapped each man as they began to settle in toward the scrub brush—covered LZ. He knew the camp's eyes were on them, the multitude of faces gradually disappearing as the Huey dropped below the roof line of the tent. He still couldn't shake his odd feeling about conducting this caliber of operation within one of the fifty states that made up America. U.S. covert operations inside her own borders . . . who'd have ever thought?

The Huey bumped against the frozen earth as the skids touched down. Instantly the team exited, all of them using the door nearest the tent which housed Billings. The pilot cut the super-charged turbine's power while Hartung and the crew chief began rigging the extra SAW so it could be used if necessary. No one spoke or exchanged greetings until the entire group had entered the tent. Billings held the flap open for them. Once they were inside, he relinquished the doorway to one of the DELTA guards, a bunker of a man who carried an H & K MP5 submachine gun as if it were a child's squirt gun.

Bailey signaled the head narc aside as the team began unzipping flight bags and removing their equipment and uniforms. Thornton himself was already seated on one of the cots provided, his tiger-stripe fatigues unfolded beside him as he prepared to change. "How we looking?" asked the young agent.

"Good," replied Billings. "I've got fifty of the western seaboard's best field agents outside. They've been briefed and split into sections; all that's left to do is gear up and move out. How about you?" As he was speaking his eyes swept over the men, taking in the precise way they were preparing individually, with no direction from Thornton.

Bailey pulled his DEA Windbreaker off, dropping it on the desk Billings had been seated at moments before. "We're as ready as we'll ever be. They're going to suit up first, then Bo wants to be brought up to date on anything that's changed since the report we received this morning on the FAX. I assume our launch is still planned for zero-zero-three-zero?"

Billings nodded in the affirmative.

Both men turned as Silver spoke. "Hey, Cal! Can you give me a hand with these demo packs?"

"Yeah, no sweat, Jason. Just a sec." Returning his attention to Billings, he got the nod to go ahead, the senior agent asking only one question. "They gonna be able to pull it off, Calvin?"

Cal, seasoned veteran of his own battles, didn't allow himself the slightest hesitation before answering. "If they don't, there's no one else we could have picked who could have."

"A little help here, Navy!" Silver now had his entire inventory heaped on a cot. Bailey moved to where he sat and began inspecting detonators while the ex-LRRP reviewed his combat harness and its load.

Billings couldn't help but envy his subordinate's acceptance by the group. He had never been in the military, choosing years ago to serve his country as one of its federal agents. Watching Bailey exchanging suggestions and lighthearted jabs of humor with Silver, he realized that the tough little agent was as at home in this environment as Billings himself was alien to it. Sadly he had to acknowledge that his kind of warrior had been beaten. Something new, something extraordinary had to be brought into play if they were going to regain the offensive.

It looked as if it would be a new breed of drug warrior, like

Bailey, they'd have to turn to if there was to be a glimmer of victory ever again. As for Thornton and his team, Billings was counting on them to give him his best Christmas.

For nearly an hour he watched as they went about their deadly business. Suddenly, as if on cue, the tent's activity came to a halt. Billings did not recognize the same group of men who had entered the dark tent earlier. What he now saw was a team of professional combat soldiers, their taut figures wrapped in soft camouflage material. In their hands they held the tools of their fatal trade. Thornton himself with his stubby Colt carbine, its brutal black muffler promising a silent death, Lee and Silver, face to face so that they could inspect each other's combat loads. Slung behind them with muzzles down were the laser-guided Minimis, a dull sheen reflecting off their oiled surfaces. Strapped under Silver's left armpit was his silenced S & W 645. Lee preferred to wear his own handgun slung low on his hip in an SAS Cordura holster. Both men, in fact all of them, Billings noted, wore long-bladed sheath knives. His skin rippled at the thought of such a knife being used within perhaps a few short hours.

He himself had shot at men over the years, had even killed several, although he wasn't particularly proud of it. But never had he consciously determined to bury a length of sharpened steel into a man with the intention of taking his life.

Looking at the men he'd activated less than a month earlier, there existed no doubt in his mind that they would not flinch if called upon to "bury it to the hilt" as the old mountain men used to say. For a split second he felt sorry for Dancer and his people. They were expecting Santa Claus but they were going to get "Hell's Own" instead.

Thornton rose, indicating to Billings that he was ready to proceed with their final briefing. The men arranged themselves so that they could continue working on the odds and ends of their gear, already well versed in the night's coming operation. Billings took his place in front of them, his concentration dispelled for just a moment as Lee pressed the button to his laser, sending its beam dancing around the canvas walls.

"Gentlemen," he began once the dot vanished. "In a few short hours you will be moved by vehicle to your objective.

At the same time the support unit will depart to take up their positions outside the target area. As of seventeen thirty hours there have been no changes to the mission."

Billings turned and picked up a handwritten list from the table at his side. "We now have all of the primary targets on site. In addition, there are approximately an equal number of female guests, and an additional six to eight bodyguards. With the twelve security personnel reported registered by the county three weeks ago, that translates to nearly thirty-five people on the property."

"Any civilians?" It was Lee, who was now beginning to apply dark greasepaint like that used by bow hunters to his face.

"None. Dancer released the entire resort's staff earlier today. When you arrive there should be only him and his people there."

"Any rumblings from local law enforcement?" This time Hartung was asking the question.

Billings pulled up a folding chair and sat. "I was in meetings with the state, county, and city earlier today. They have been told that this is strictly a federal operation due to suspected leaks in their organizations. They are highly pissed, but they have no choice but to stay clear of us. We'll handle their feelings afterward."

Thornton now stood, his appearance substantially altered from his initial meeting with Billings because of the tiger-striped uniform, camo greasepaint and the harness full of weaponry which hung from his powerful shoulders. "We plan to move by foot through the tree line until we hit the helicopters. Silver will wire them up as well as the transformer behind the main building. Once that's finished we'll enter the grounds and move to the main entrance. Jason will blow the transformer, cutting off all the power to the premises.

"At that time we'll enter the building and move to the basement, where the lab is. While Lee and I secure the area, Jason will place the rest of his explosives. We'll also terminate any lab personnel we encounter. Because we're utilizing remote detonators for the choppers, the lab charges will be blown, using time pencils."

"How much time will that allow you to clear the lab?" asked Bailey.

"Three minutes after I've broken the pencils," replied Silver. "Once the charges are set, there's no way to stop the firing sequence. Everything will be daisy-chained together as well as independently wired. That will ensure *something* going off regardless of what happens to us before or after."

Thornton resumed his briefing. "We intend to exit through the delivery door located at the rear of the lab. From there we'll E-and-E over the fence and begin moving toward our PZ."

"That's where me and the chopper will extract," grunted Hartung. "In the meantime I'll be flying a three hundred sixty–degree orbit several miles out, ready to yank 'em if things go to shit right off the bat."

"What if their choppers get airborne during the assault?" queried Billings.

Thornton replied. "Both Frank and Jason have remote transmitters. If the Bells lift off we'll blow them in flight, depending on what actions the pilots take."

Billings signaled his approval of the plan with an upturned thumb.

"We'll be in constant communication with each other during the operation," continued Thornton. "I would prefer everyone stay off the net except for the aircrew and ourselves. It'll be chaotic enough without trying to carry on a running commentary with anybody else.

"We do not intend to look for Dancer or his people. If any of them become targets of opportunity, naturally we'll engage. Our plan is to get inside both quickly and silently, rig the lab, then use the resulting explosion to terminate the entire target folder."

For several moments after he had stopped speaking, everyone was silent. Then Billings spoke. "We'll wait until we hear you're clear of the area before we move in to clean up." Looking at the pilot, he said, "Your orders are to return the team here. Medical support will be standing by if necessary. Either Calvin or myself will cut you loose to return to the coast once we've determined the extent of your success. From there you'll stand by for at least forty-eight hours. After that, you're on your own."

The men acknowledged the senior DEA officer's mandate with either a nod of a head or a grunt.

"Frank, check everyone's gear one more time, to include mine," barked Thornton. Turning to his team, the former One-Zero locked his eyes into theirs. "Everybody racks out until Frank and I get you up. You need anything, ask Calvin for it. In the meantime get all the rest you can . . . we're gonna need it."

Turning to Billings and motioning him outside, Thornton spun on his heel and left the tent. He'd only taken a few steps into the cool night air before he heard the agent's footsteps echoing his own in the delicate layer of snow that had fallen. Drawing in a deep breath of air, he waited to speak until he felt Billings standing next to him. "That's a lot of guns we're going in against, you know."

Billings kicked at the snow, his breath forming dual jets of misty vapor as he exhaled through his nose. "Calvin says you're the best."

Thornton laughed. "Yeah, well that boy ain't been right since he hit his head on one of the mines we dropped in Danny Ortega's backyard."

"You feeling okay about this?" asked Billings.

Thornton slipped his hand into his combat tunic to adjust the sheath of his springblade so that it sat further forward on his belt. "You just be ready to pick up the pieces when we're done. And make sure my people's money is in the bank by close of business tomorrow. They'll have earned it."

Billings grunted his assent. "Nice night for it," he offered.

Thornton looked up. Before he turned to go, he reached over and shook the DEA man's hand. "They call it a hunter's moon where I come from."

Billings stayed outside until the cold drove him to the tent.

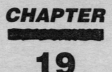

Hartung moved among the men like a wraith, his powerful fingers gently prodding them awake, one by one. Thornton was already up and sitting with Bailey and Billings, hot mugs of caffeine-rich coffee and adrenaline encouraging a motor-mouthed conversation. Within minutes the team moved silently in preparation. Having slept in their uniforms, they needed only to slip on their boots before being ready for some coffee themselves. The aircrew had been awakened thirty minutes earlier and were outside pulling their preflight checks on the Huey.

The steady roar of the camp's portable generators masked the noises made by an army of DEA agents. Car doors were opened and engines started as the order was issued to begin deployment. Men hurried from their tents carrying weapons, portable lights, evidence containers, medical kits, and zip-lock body bags. From the communications truck flowed a current of radio transmissions sent by teams entering the operational frequency. Out on the perimeter DELTA teams checked in with each other, using their own internal radios. So far the only activity they had to report was taking place inside the mission support site itself.

Back in the tent the men conducted final inspections. Bailey collected their personal items, except for their watches, which were synchronized against Thornton's Rolex. Once that was done they began testing the team's radios. With headbands securing the light weight ear pieces in place, each man exited the tent and contacted both Thornton and Hartung. Satisfied that they had five-by communications, the commandos turned to their individual weapons. Lee and Silver removed the eight AA batteries that powered their lasers, replacing them with fresh ones. Thornton sprayed several drops of WD40 into his carbine's trigger mechanism, then removed the weapon's original suppressor, replacing it with his secondary unit.

Finished with their lasers, his teammates hefted their squad automatic weapons and adjusted each gun's assault sling to his individual liking. Running the bolts back and forth, they assured themselves that each SAW was functioning perfectly.

Hartung reappeared at their sides; hung over his shoulder were their specially designed combat vests "borrowed" from SEAL Team 8's special-ops inventory. Each vest carried four 200-round boxes of 5.56 linked ammunition to be carried for the SAWs, as well as grenades, extra pistol magazines, first-aid packs, and knives. Thornton wore the standard-issue LBE harness, but like Silver he carried a butt pack in which was packed their demolitions equipment.

Finishing their adjustments, each man double-checked the other's work. To be successful they would have to move silently and yet be able to retrieve any item of equipment without a second's delay.

"Ready for the goggles, Bo?"

"Sure, Frank. Everyone draw your five-hundred and load 'em with fresh batteries. Function check in five minutes, everybody out back with me." Taking his own pair from the sergeant major's outstretched hand, Thornton grabbed the necessary batteries and locked them into their individual compartments. Hearing the slight purr of the set as he activated the "on" switch, he slipped the goggles onto his head, adjusting the flexible strap so that they fit comfortably over his eyes. Satisfied, he jacked a round into his pistol's breech and double-checked the Hi-Power's magazines. He'd humped a Browning during both his tours with SOG and liked the way the gun took care of business. Thornton didn't care much about ballistics tests . . . he always double-tapped his target regardless of caliber. The object of pulling the trigger was to ventilate with extreme accuracy; anything else was half-stepping.

The others were quick to follow. Once outside they adjusted the goggles over their eyes and, at Thornton's command, turned them on. The night's winter darkness was dispelled. With amazing clarity they were able to see each other's features, and looking toward the chopper, they quietly observed the crew as they went about their business. Suddenly both groups were staring at each other, the spell broken as one of the pilots flipped Thornton's team the bird.

"The van's ready," advised Bailey from the tent's opening.

"Frank?"

"Yeah, Bo."

"We'll see you on the ground. You got all your shit?"

Hartung, dressed in an Army nomex flight suit borrowed from one of the pilots, answered. "Roger that. I'll keep you advised from the air. If either of Dancer's choppers go airborne, I'll let you know."

Both men stared hard at each other, then clasped hands. "Take care, partner," whispered Hartung. "Remember, you ain't as young as you used to be!"

Thornton grinned. "Just don't fall outta the damn bird, you old fart . . . and let the pilots do their job! The last thing they need tonight is a backseat driver."

With that, Hartung grabbed his own SAW, and with a wave of his hand headed for the Huey's squat form.

"Let's do it," ordered Thornton.

Leaving the van, they moved quickly into the protective concealment of the forest, moving silently by foot to their objective. Thornton took point, anxious to get them away from the highway and any late-night travelers who might by chance catch them in their headlights. The goggles made movement effortless through the silent trees. When he'd covered a hundred meters by his own pace count he stopped, whispering into his mike for Lee to come forward.

For the next forty-five minutes they didn't move. No one spoke as they willed themselves to become a part of the night. Comfortable as they were with the goggles, it was still weird being able to see everything but not be seen themselves. Checking his Submariner, Thornton nudged Lee and signaled him to begin their trek toward the resort. The others carefully boosted themselves up off the ground, their pants wet from where their rumps had thawed the frozen earth.

Twenty minutes later Lee stopped them. It was just after two in the morning and the sky was filled with stars so bright they seemed on fire. A slight breeze hurried through the trees, its movement causing their empty branches to quiver. To their front they saw the two Bell helicopters sitting by themselves in a pool of yellow light. Fifty meters away was a small hangar, its single light bathing the grounds in a weak glow. They watched for any sign of a guard on patrol. After five minutes, Thornton concluded that the guards were merely making spot checks of the chopper pad, then hurrying back to the comfort of the hangar. Thornton spoke softly into his mike.

"Lee, see if you can't work your way around back of the hangar and over to the transformer. Once you're there you should be able to cover Jason from that side of the clearing. How copy?"

Lee touched Thornton's arm in acknowledgment, then rose to a half-crouch and moved towards the building. They were able to follow his progress until he turned its corner, seconds later reappearing and moving quickly until he gained the cover of the metal power source. "In position whenever you're ready," murmured the sniper.

Pulling the Minimi's stock close into his side and holding it by the pistol grip, Silver made one last visual recon of the clearing before beginning to cross it. He felt completely vulnerable, but reminded himself that he was invisible to anyone not having their own night-vision equipment. Even if one of the guards cared enough to make a cursory check, the man's night-vision would be gone after sitting in a lighted room. Still, the very act of walking across a danger zone as if he were going for a Sunday paper caused the demo man's hackles to rise in rigid protest.

Reaching the first chopper, he crouched down in relief and sucked in several deep breaths. Making a quick visual check, he pulled one of the prepared charges from his combat tunic and fastened it underneath the body of the Bell's passenger compartment. Removing the safety clip from the toggle switch, he pushed it forward and watched as the detonator's

green light began to softly glow. Satisfied that the charge was
armed, Silver whispered that he was finished and began to
move toward the second airship. Hearing an all-clear from
both Lee and Thornton, he gingerly picked his way through
the snow, the SAW now firmly gripped in both his hands, its
safety off.

He was just finishing attaching the second charge when a
shaft of light spilled out from the hangar's door. "Trouble!"
exclaimed Lee. "Dig a hole, Jason, you got company comin'
from your eleven o'clock!"

Thornton watched as the guard stepped into his field of vision.
The man's weapon hung from a sling over his shoulder, and as
he zipped his parka closed he turned and spoke to someone
still inside the heated building. A rattle of laughter echoed
across the snowy clearing, then the door shut and the guard
was alone. With a quick stamp of his feet he began a slow
walk toward the first helicopter; nothing in his manner indicated that he expected to find anything out of the ordinary.

"Where is he?" hissed Jason.

Lee answered. "By the first chopper you rigged. He's just
walking around it now. Wait a minute. Okay, now he's checking the doors . . . pilot side first. Hey, where the hell are you?"

Silver's voice was barely audible. "I'm in the damn bird.
The passenger door was unlocked. What the fuck's he doing
now?"

Thornton listened to Lee as the man described the guard's
movements step by anxious step. Turning his silenced carbine's snout toward the hangar, he readied himself to waste
anyone who stepped outside.

"He's headed your way, my man," whispered Lee.

Inside the frigid cockpit, Silver slipped the big 645 clear of its
holster and thumbed the hammer back. Hoping the man
wouldn't notice the SAW left on the inside of the Bell's skid,
he braced himself in expectation of the door opening once the
man twisted its unlocked handle.

The guard dutifully paced off the perimeter of the ship,
oblivious to Silver's tracks. Reaching the pilot's door, he gave
the handle a quick tug, satisfied when it remained shut. Shuf-

fling around the nose of the aircraft, he failed to notice the nickel-sized red dot that materialized against his jacket from the direction of the transformer. It disappeared as he stepped up to the passenger door, his gloved hand grasping the handle and giving it a sharp twist.

As the door popped open, Silver registered the surprised man's reaction as he began squeezing the .45's trigger. Without thought he adjusted the aim of the silenced automatic so that the subsonic round impacted directly between the startled guard's eyes. Halfway through the man's skull, the Silver Tip began to expand, finally reaching a .60-caliber diameter before exiting out the back of his now-shattered brain housing group. From the cover of the trees, Thornton watched the body attempt a poor imitation of Michael Jackson's famous Moonwalk before it crumpled to the ground. Seconds later, Silver hopped from the Bell, pumping a second brain emulsifier into the inert corpse's cranium.

"Bingo!" snapped Silver. "How we lookin'?"

"We got the barn covered, Jay, just do your thing and get the hell over here," commanded Lee.

Silver lifted the lifeless carcass into the Bell's cockpit and carefully closed the door. Working quickly, he fixed the second block of C-4 to the chopper's belly, retrieving the SAW only after he'd assured himself that the detonator was functioning properly. Noticing Lee waving to him, Silver jogged over to where the man knelt.

"Okay, Bo, your turn," whispered Lee.

Thornton slipped his thumb over the carbine's safety and stood. Taking a deep breath, he moved at a steady pace across the clearing and into the wood line, where Lee and Silver were hidden. Turning to face the hangar, all three men waited, half expecting the dead guard's partner to appear in the doorway. When it didn't happen they relaxed for a moment, then took stock of their situation.

"The transformer?" questioned Thornton.

"It's already wired. I worked up a mini platter charge back at the MSS. That should smoke it something fierce. I rigged a five-minute pencil on her; that'll cut it close but we ain't here to exchange Christmas cards, anyway."

"What about the other guard?" asked Lee.

"He's either asleep or they've got a timed routine for the watch. In any case he's not going to be concerned about his buddy once that pencil shuts everything down. Let's get inside." Motioning Lee to once again take point, Thornton tapped Silver on the back before he moved. "Nice work with the guard, Jay, very clean."

The demo specialist grinned, then chased Lee's rapidly moving form. The team hadn't covered twenty meters before they reached the servant's gate. Surprised, they noted that it was wide open, the lock and chain wrapped so that it wouldn't close in the wind. "Someone isn't too concerned with our being here," observed Lee.

"It's definitely Christmas," marveled Thornton. "Must have left it open so they wouldn't have to worry about passing off the key when they changed shifts."

Lee started forward, his Minimi's barrel now swinging from left to right as he entered the heart of Alpine. Assuming a half-crouch, he crept along the dimly lit sidewalk, stopping every few meters to listen for anyone approaching from the other direction.

"Two minutes 'til showtime, Dave, let's pick up the pace," urged Thornton.

Looking toward the huge lodge, they saw lights burning throughout the second floor, as well as on the third. Strains of music escaped from several half-open windows, a man's laughter erupting above them, causing all three commandos to step quickly into the safety of the trees. A moment later, a glass shattered against the poured concrete, followed by a woman's throaty chuckle.

"Their party's about to end, and ours is about to start . . . so let's get our asses around the front, shall we?"

Acknowledging Thornton's voice, Lee stepped onto the sidewalk and boldly moved out. Gritting his teeth, he loped ahead, stopping when he reached the near corner of the building. Scanning the area off to his left to make sure it was clear, he led the team down the length of the building. They had just reached the far corner when the night's quiet was fragmented by the painful detonation of Silver's charge gutting the transformer into thousands of pieces of useless technology.

For a fraction of a moment the lights along the walkway
fluttered in a hopeful attempt to stay alive. They failed. Behind the team a small fire began burning where the transformer had stood. The night's holy stillness was once again
broken as the sound of panicked men came from the open
windows. Women began shouting in a vain attempt to understand the sudden change of atmosphere. A beam of light
pierced the clearing where the helicopters stood. The remaining guard and the Bell's pilots cautiously moved toward the
site of the explosion, weapons in their hands.

"Party's over," observed Thornton.

Taking the stairs two at a time, Lee mounted the porch and
moved rapidly toward the lodge's twin doors. As he reached
them a man dressed in a Santa suit pushed his way outside, a
pistol in one hand and a long black flashlight in the other.
Before Lee could react to the bizarre sight he felt the sputter of
Thornton's Colt next to his neck. The suppressed weapon
blew away the man's face in a thunderous spray of shredded
flesh and white bone, leaving behind a broken bowl full of
cranial cole slaw.

Quickly taking the point, Thornton grabbed hold of one
of the heavy doors and pushed it open. Even though the
electricity had been cut, battery-powered emergency lights
provided a ghostly illumination throughout the lodge. From
upstairs he could hear the sounds of people moving, long
beams of white light showing that partygoers had armed
themselves with flashlights. Angry voices collided with each
other as Thornton guided the team into the unlocked stairwell leading to the lab.

Moments after they'd gained the questionable safety of the
stairs, there was a rush of feet as Stennmaker's troops headed
for the porch. The first two men tripped over the dead Santa's
body as they burst through the doors.

Stennmaker himself landed hard, his momentum carrying
him several feet past the nearly headless body. Playing his
light's powerful beam over it, he gagged as he saw what
Thornton's 9mm galvanizers had done to the once-handsome
face. Pulling himself up on one knee, he snatched his Motorola from its keeper and keyed it. "Magnumson! You copy?"

"Shit yes! Tony wants to know what the hell is going on . . . ?"

"I got a very dead Santa's brains smeared all over the porch and no lights to work by. Hold one while I talk with the chopper pad. . . ."

Before he could make contact Stennmaker heard the muffled staccato of a machine gun, gushing from deep within the lodge. All at once his radio was overpowered with broken transmissions as everyone attempted to discover what was happening. Throwing the instrument down in disgust, he grabbed the man next to him and ordered everyone back into the house. Idiots! he raged to himself. So much for hiring professionals! What the hell was going on?

Entering the basement's foyer Thornton emptied his first magazine into what had been the lab's sole protector. The man had met them at the door, apparently believing they were his own people. Stepping over the scrapped body, the men hurried to the lab's heavy metal entrance. From behind it they heard people frantically arguing. Lee moved up, banging the butt of his SAW against the door, and ordered the occupants to open up. As the lock was turned he violently twisted the knob and pushed inward. Confronted by a pair of shocked eyes belonging to one of the chemists, he jammed his Minimi's barrel into the man's face and squeezed a long burst of tracer fire through it.

Stepping back to allow Thornton to kick the door fully open, both men braced themselves against the wall as Silver rolled a Stingball riot grenade into the lab. The explosion sprayed 150 hard plastic balls the size of double-aught buck throughout the room. The two remaining chemists who'd been spared Lee's initial volley pled for mercy as they were struck by the hard-hitting pellets.

Leaping into the dimly lit laboratory, Thornton ordered Lee to cover the team while Silver began unloading his charges. Jerking the two whimpering drug makers up, Thornton pushed and kicked them toward a corner of the room while checking to see if anyone else was there. Beside himself with fear, one of the chemists attempted to escape from Thornton's grip. For this mistake he was treated to a three-round burst from the night raider's carbine. Stepping back to watch the man's body bounce off the wall, Thornton turned his demonic suppressor on the remaining "cooker" and emptied the weapon on full auto.

Behind him he heard Lee shout a warning, then was deafened as the SAW began hammering out a steady stream of steel into the first of Stennmaker's men on the scene. Turning, he saw Silver place a round plastique charge against one of the huge stainless steel vats of what Bailey had said were pure P_2P, the primary chemical necessary for the production of methamphetamine. Lee stopped firing for the moment, his voice crackling inside Thornton's head. "We better get moving, people! I just smoked a load of folks comin' down the stairs, but it ain't over yet. Where are we, Bo?"

"Jay?"

"Almost finished, Sarge. Shit, there's a ton of chemicals down here. I can see what looks like a vault over to my left, and there's a bunch of packages next to our exit point."

Lee's Minimi opened up again, its high-pitched ripping howl combining with the clatter of expended brass. Powder smoke was filling up the room, thick cordite coating their tongues and making it hard to breathe. "Help me get this bastard closed!" yelled the gunner as bullets began whacking into the half-open security door. Thornton grimaced as sparks flew from the door and showered Lee's prostrate figure. Low-crawling as quickly as he could, Thornton reached the door and shoved it closed, allowing Lee to roll back into the laboratory. Abruptly it was quiet except for their ragged breathing and the faint sound of men running toward their now-locked entrance.

Upstairs Tony Dancer gathered everyone into the large living room of his spacious quarters. The roar of automatic-weapons fire could be clearly heard below them. Magnumson had taken two of Stennmaker's people as he attempted to find out what was happening. Looking out one of his favorite bay windows, Dancer was dismayed not to see a horde of flashing blue lights, which would have indicated that the DEA finally decided to take their best shot. If the cops weren't downstairs then it had to be someone who was as outside the law as Tony Dancer himself . . . and that meant a hit was going down. Spinning back toward those assembled in the room, he examined their faces in the glow of the candles he'd ordered lit.

"Which one of you treacherous assholes called this one?" he said, a tone of mild rebuke in his voice.

Before any of them could protest, Magnumson burst back into the room, his .380 gripped tightly in his hand. "Tony! Whoever they are, we got 'em buttoned up in the lab. I sent Stennmaker around back to seal it off."

Dancer pursed his lips in thought. When he spoke his voice was like ice. "We've got to get them out of that lab without too much damage. I'm coming down, Mag, have someone watch our friends here . . . I wouldn't want anything to happen to them while I'm gone!"

As the group began to protest Dancer's obvious accusation, he turned to leave. Glancing toward the half-open sliding glass door, he was stunned to see what appeared to be a bear holding a weapon in its paw standing under one of the outdoor emergency lights. With a gasp of adrenaline-enhanced fear, Dancer leaped past Magnumson just as the Monk began spraying the room's interior with steel-jacketed slugs. Any order that was left among the guests collapsed as quickly as did the custom glass portal when the 5.56 spine-busters screamed into the crowded room.

Magnumson snapped two ill-aimed shots in the general direction of where the Monk was standing, one of them intercepting Barf Bag Suddath as he tried to escape the line of fire.

After witnessing the explosion and seeing the lights go dead, the bikers immediately ran up the outside stairwell to the third-floor sun deck. Monk ignored the sounds of gunfire from the other end of the building, his only intention being to find Dancer and waste him. Clambering onto the flat expanse, he'd waited until the others were beside him before crawling toward the group of people assembled in the huge room. He was just drawing a bead on Dancer himself when the man spun on his heel to leave, throwing the half-sane biker's aim off as he pulled the trigger.

With a roar, the Monk emptied his thirty-round load into the room, his companions lining up alongside him and working the actions of their own weapons as fast as possible.

The noise was beyond deafening. Ragged hunks of furniture flew apart as double-aught buckshot ripped into chairs, sofas, and tables. Lampshades were shredded by broken bits of spring steel, bulbs exploding under the impact of high-velocity lead. Dancer's carefully selected paintings, struck by the barrage of gunfire, became broken children's puzzles. On the floor, people rolled, crawling, screaming, crying, shouting, and, every so often, dying. It was as if they were inside the ultimate popcorn popper, and they were the kernels.

Gehlen spotted his informant as she vigorously crawled over the glass-infested carpet toward where Magnumson was now kneeling, his handgun replaced by the MAC .380. Shouldering the H & K Super 90, the biker screamed her name as loud as he could, hoping to draw her attention. When she failed to hesitate, as he had hoped, he began yanking the trigger, causing massive chunks of flooring to disintegrate all around the girl as the shotgunner attempted to bring her down. When she reached Magnumson, he grabbed a handful of long, loose blond hair and jerked her bodily into the safety of the hall. Triggering a fast burst toward where the murderous biker had been standing seconds before, the former Marine turned to his now hysterical girl friend and yelled for her to regain control.

"You're okay, bitch! Shut up and get a grip!" Searching the nylon bag at his side, he found a full magazine of .380 eye-poppers and reloaded the now-empty MAC.

"That was that crazy, creepy biker asshole, Gehlen," sobbed the girl. "He tried to kill me, Mag! He promised me that he'd leave me alone!" Her face was now buried in her cut and bleeding hands, the once-revealing dress she was wearing now covered with bits of sofa stuffing and other people's blood.

Magnumson stared hard at the woman, then ripped her hands away from her face, shoving his own directly into it. "You *know* one of those bastards?" he yelled. The stoned-out, beat-up, half-coherent farm girl from Lander, Wyoming could only nod dumbly.

"Kill her," ordered Dancer. The cartel's kingpin sat several feet away, a large-bore magnum in his hand.

Grabbing the girl by her ears, Magnumson threw her back into the killing grounds. As she bounced off the edge of the once-ornate dining table, Gehlen spotted her and fired from the hip. His aim held true, catching the blond just as she began to fall to the floor. As her hip exploded in a spray of fatty tissue and body fluid, Magnumson stitched a twelve-round pattern into the strapless evening dress. Flinching under the thunderous bellow of Dancer's magnum, he then watched as Terri's head fragmented like a piece of dropped crystal, the heavy-caliber bullet exiting through her forehead and burying itself in the opposite wall.

The firefight had taken its toll.

The "Pointer" had taken a wicked beating from a Satan's Rebels Uzi, his legs nearly severed at the knees. Several feet away lay his girl friend of the weekend, a teenage model marketed by a mother who had hopes of a fat contract with *Miss Teen Magazine* if her daughter could please the San Francisco deviate. LaPoneta's own bodyguard had found cover next to a heavy table and just cranked three rounds from his Smith and Wesson Model 60 into Gehlen's body.

Dancer's date pulled herself underneath one of the couches, and although unwounded she screamed into the thick carpet. Nazi Bill had just churned Willy Granger's entrails into mush with a full-auto burst when Jerry Graves from Alaska hit him across the back of the head with the oak cane he habitually carried. The skinny biker's skull oozed a steady flow of blood onto the carpet; a long shank of window glass had punctured his cheek and entered his brain's cortex, ensuring his death.

The Monk felt the tide of battle turning against him, and as he slammed a fresh magazine into the smoking Colt, he began yelling to what was left of his force to pull back onto the outside deck. In the hallway, Magnumson had just received reinforcements from downstairs and was preparing to reenter the room. Stennmaker had kept two men outside the lab's door, where Thornton was held up, and ordered two others to cover the emergency exit. As the bikers began rushing back into the cold night's air, those inside who were still alive began screaming for help.

Magnumson led the charge, his MAC sending long bursts through the already-tattered curtains. Behind him came the others, their guns providing a steel screen of covering fire as they took up positions in the now-devastated room. On the deck itself lay the Monk and two survivors of the assault. Unable to return to the stairwell they had climbed only minutes earlier, the bikers lay belly down against the astro-carpeted decking, their supply of ammunition dwindling as they attempted to keep the now-eager attackers inside the resort.

In the lab, Thornton watched as Silver finished rigging his charges. Tying the last length of det-cord off, he swiftly stuffed the remainder of his equipment into an olive green satchel and turned toward his team leader. "Okay, we're set. I set 'em with five-minute delays instead of three, just in case it takes us longer to clear the AO."

Thornton nodded his agreement. They hadn't heard anything outside the main door since somebody had yelled about needing more men upstairs. Lee moved to the rear of the lab and now stood by the exit, his Minimi reloaded and off safe as he prepared to lead them out.

"Viper One, this is Springblade. Over."

Twenty-five hundred feet above the ground, Frank Hartung slapped the crew chief hard on the back as he heard his partner's voice. "Springblade—I have you five-by, how me?"

"I have you same. Stand by to meet us at the PZ in five mikes. We have no WIA or KIA at this time. Over."

"Roger that, Springblade. Beginning our approach at this time. Keep us informed as you break contact. Over."

"You'll be the first to know, Viper."

Three miles away, Bailey gave Billings a relieved grin. The two narcs had been going crazy listening to the assault as it unfolded. Everywhere along the highway DEA agents were chomping at the bit to crash the party. Billings alerted them to prepare to move out on his command.

Thornton removed his already-fresh magazine from the now-quiet carbine and checked its load. Satisfied, he clicked it back into place and then touched his Randall's butt cap. He felt the springblade's presence against his hip bone, where it hung on his black garrison belt. Casting an inquisitive eye toward Silver, he received a curt nod. The LRRP was ready. Moving to where Lee stood waiting, the One-Zero tapped him lightly on the shoulder.

Lee braced the Minimi against his hip and with one hand on its pistol grip, he reached forward with the other and carefully depressed the door's release bar. The exit opened a fraction, its hinges popping as the door's weight snapped the crust of ice that had formed on them. Lee stopped. For the first time they could hear the intensity of the firefight. Exchanging confused looks, Thornton ordered Lee to open the door further, both men preparing to leap back inside should they come under fire.

The stairwell leading upward to freedom was deserted.

Signaling Lee to close the door, Thornton directed Silver to arm the charges. "Jay, fire 'em up and let's get the hell out of here. I don't know what all that other shit is, but we'd better get clear before they come back for us."

Silver ran back into the lab and one by one depressed the time pencils' activators. Within seconds he was back. "Time to blow this pop stand, if you'll pardon the pun. She's counting."

Lee shoved the door open and began climbing the stairs, his laser boring a red hole in the night's chill air. The point man hadn't reached the third step when a fusillade of shotgun blasts tore down the passageway, the heavy steel pellets careening throughout the narrow confines of the stairwell, striking Lee in the legs and lower torso. "Shit! Shit! Shit!" he screamed as his finger tightened around the Minimi's trigger. A long burst of machine-gun fire swept upward, drowning out the continuing fire from the trees nearest the exit. Thornton grabbed the wounded man and pulled him into the safety of the lab.

"They musta heard us open the door the first time and were just waiting for us to leave," cursed Lee.

"How bad you hit?" asked Thornton.

"Feels like the lower calves took some buck, maybe a few in my gut."

Thornton cursed inwardly. "Can you walk?" His point man nodded briskly.

Silver turned from his position at the door. "Bo, we gotta move and I mean *now*! Once the pencils are cracked that's it . . . unless I tear everything apart."

"That ain't gonna happen!" snarled Thornton. "Jay, hit his

calves with the Ace wraps, one per." Silver scooted across the floor, ripping into his chest pack for the first aid items. "Viper One! You got a copy on me?"

Hartung's voice was immediately present. "Yeah, Bo . . . what the hell's the problem? Is Lee okay?"

"He can move," responded Thornton. "I got about four minutes before this place turns to cinders. They've blocked our exit, but if you can give me some cover fire we should be able to break outta here."

"It's on the way! Toss me some Chem-Lites so I can mark my zone, how copy?"

Silver was already pulling six-inch plastic lights from one of his harness pouches. Rapidly cracking the tubes so that the two chemicals inside could interact, he bundled them together and headed back to the exit. Lee finished the wrap job on his seeping legs, a steady stream of Spanish expletives punctuating his efforts to stem the flow of blood pooling underneath him.

"Let's ditch these goggles and radios," ordered Thornton. The men removed their electronic equipment, shoving the now-unnecessary gear into the cargo pockets of their fatigue pants.

Thornton alone had commo with the bird. "Frank?" he murmured.

"Go ahead, Bo."

"Jay's gonna toss the sticks. Even if you don't see them give us everything you can for about thirty seconds. After that head for the PZ. If we ain't there most *rickety-tick* . . ."

"Hey, fuck that kinda talk, asshole!" snapped Hartung. "I'm gonna waste every dick-lickin' son of a bitch within fifty meters of that door. You people just move your asses when you hear us pull off. How copy?"

Thornton grinned. "That's a solid copy, Sergeant Major. We're lighting the Christmas tree now."

Pointing to Silver, he watched as the toughest little bastard he'd ever served with kicked the door's locking bar, sending the metal aperture flying open. Again the stairwell was flooded with gunfire from the outer darkness. Shouting an unintelligible oath at the hidden gunmen, Silver heaved the Chem-Lites up and over the narrow passage's wall. Overhead they could hear the steady beat of the Huey, knowing Hartung now leaned out over the skid, preparing to douse the tract of ground around the exit with his SAW.

"I gotcha now!" bellowed Hartung. Thornton tore his own radio from his head, stuffing the device into the opposite cargo pocket from where he's stored his goggles.

"Fire in the hole!" he yelled as the first rounds began to impact against the building. All three men tucked themselves up against the near wall, each of them shaking with powerful surges of adrenaline as they counted down the seconds before they could leave the protection of the time bomb they now occupied.

Outside the gunship was in a near hover, Hartung swung the SAW in a methodical arc as he walked his rounds into a figure that exploded into view. He grunted in satisfaction as the burst met the man in the upper chest, knocking him backward into the tree line. Sensing another breaking cover, the sergeant major asked for altitude and managed to zip the desperately weaving man as he ran for a shallow culvert that meandered throughout the wooded grounds. "That's it!" he cheered, his gloved hand alerting the crew chief that they could break away and run for the PZ.

Hearing the chopper veering away from them, Thornton cinched his Colt's frame in tight to his body and gave the word. "Let's do it, people!" he yelled. "If we ain't halfway to Cleveland in about two minutes we're dog meat!"

With a guttural profanity, Lee pitched himself up the stairs, his Minimi's barrel turning white-hot as the linked belt of organ grinders sped their way down the tube. Behind hopped Silver, his own SAW going into battery once Lee was clear of its savage snout. Taking two steps at a time, Thornton bounded up behind his surging team, bellowing encouragement, though no one could hear him. Running toward the far fence line, they heard two sets of rotors starting up as Dancer's air force prepared to lift off.

Behind them the final minute began its swift end.

"Tell the pilots I want them up here *now*!" ordered Dancer. Crouched in the hallway's door, Magnumson lifted the radio to his mouth and urgently relayed a set of instructions to the helipad. Satisfied at the response, he grunted, nodding to Dancer that the birds would be there within moments.

Ramming a fresh magazine into both his weapons, the former Marine signaled to the men who'd joined them from downstairs that it was time to retake lost ground. More important, they had to push the enemy not only out of the lodge itself, but off the emergency LZ before the Bells could land.

Inside the room there was a brisk exchange of gunfire as Jerry Graves, along with the remaining hardcases whose jobs it had been to protect the now dead, began to force the Monk and his bikers back into the night. The Monk himself was the first to exit, his Colt Commando chugging steadily as he backstepped onto the deck.

Under his fire crawled the remaining two bikers who had begun the attack on Alpine. As they scrambled onto the glass-covered platform they began to lay down a base of fire which would allow the Monk to reach the safety of the staircase. It was then that Magnumson rushed forward in a determined effort that added both firepower and incentive to the survivors of Dancer's party.

The biker named Lucas began to come apart at the joints as a surge of rifled steel smashed its way through his rapidly disintegrating body. His companion dropped to the deck, his Uzi choking out its last round. Behind him, the Monk clambered down the first few steps, then turned, his carbine's barrel, now resting on the lip of the platform, his finger tightening once again on its trigger. "Get your ass back here, DD!"

Risking a quick look toward where the Monk was concealed, DD racked the Uzi's bolt back. Inside the room the victors positioned themselves behind the thickest and largest of the room's furnishings, acknowledging Monk's bull-like roar by cocking their own weapons as he ordered his man back. Above the fracas they heard the powerful beat of rotors, now airborne and preparing to touch down on the resort's body-strewn roof.

"Choppers comin' in!" shouted Magnumson. "Give the bastards everything you got—we need to clear the deck before they touch down!"

The room erupted in gunfire as every armed man furiously pulled his trigger. Their target's last remaining shred of confidence evaporated as the deadly crescendo washed over him. Leaping to his booted feet and screaming in fear, the biker turned and ran for the deck's far end. Midway into his first step, he jerked with the impact of high-velocity slugs. Then suddenly it was as if he had no say in where he was headed. Bullet after speeding bullet pushed him along until there was nothing but the Monk's horrified face below, then that, too, was gone.

He fell three stories from the roof.

Several hundred feet above the melee, the first Bell activated its landing lights, illuminating the frantic biker's last few moments above earth. The pilot didn't see the Monk drop his now empty rifle and began lumbering as quickly as he could down the stairs. Neither did he notice the blacked-out Huey after it pulled away from the back of the lodge and headed toward the mountains. Magnumson clearly heard the pilot as he began his descent.

"Mr. Magnumson? This is Alpine One. Over."

Magnumson keyed his radio. "Yeah, I gotcha, Alpine One. How's it look from up there?"

"Nasty, very nasty. Where do you want me? Over."

Dancer spoke. "Tell him to set the damn bird down now.

I'm flying out with Jerry, everyone else stays. We'll alert the Lear once we're airborne."

As Magnumson relayed the message, the Bell floated into view, its rotor wash sending the debris of battle upward in a savagely swirling spiral. The second Bell turned its nose toward the direction the Huey had flown, on a brief reconnaissance ordered by the first bird's pilot.

Graves and Dancer sprinted to the waiting helicopter. They boarded as the building began to tremble when the first of Silver's charges detonated. Without further warning, the entire opposite end of Alpine exploded in a thunderclap that flattened those still in the building. Great gouts of flame shot into the sky, their fury sucking up whatever oxygen there was. As the structure began to shudder in the aftermath of the secondary chemical explosions, Dancer's Bell leaped skyward.

The team was inside the tree line, running for the far fence. Lee's wounds didn't seem to bother him as he pushed his way through the snow and low shrubbery. Silver stayed close to him, his internal clock rapidly counting down the final seconds before the first blast. Above they heard the Bells as they swept toward the rooftop. The DEA chopper was now several klicks out, preparing for the team's extraction. Thornton jogged several meters behind his two comrades, his combat senses on red alert.

Suddenly the night was torn asunder as the lab vaporized in a torrent of smoke and raw flames. The blast's concussion was so powerful it blew the fleeing men off their feet as it hammered through the trees.

Attempting to burrow into the frozen ground, they were showered by broken bits and pieces of their night's work. When the downpour of ash and trash had subsided, Thornton ordered them forward.

The woods took on a hellish cast in the dancing flames of Alpine. Thornton turned and scanned the area to their rear as Silver helped Lee cross the narrow culvert that ran through the property. Climbing up the shallow ditch, they disappeared into the juniper shrubs on the opposite side.

• • •

Then the Night Stalker himself turned and slipped into the trench.

Thornton felt the man's rush against his back an instant before impact drove him face first into the opposite bank. In that split second he was able to position his hands so that he could propel himself away from the frigid ground as his attacker locked a brutal forearm around his throat. Pedaling backward in the narrow confines of the ditch, Thornton felt the viselike choke hold loosen as he slammed the man's spine against the lip of the opposite wall.

Taking advantage of the lull, Bo threw his hip slightly to the left, at the same time driving his right elbow hard into the unprotected belly of his assailant. This time there was an audible groan as the man released his tenuous grip on Thornton, pushing away to put distance between them.

Spinning on the balls of both feet and dropping into a low fighting stance, Thornton pulled his carbine's stock up underneath his arm and pulled the trigger. It was only then that he realized he'd emptied the entire magazine during the team's breakout minutes earlier and not replaced it.

Flipping the short rifle behind him so it hung by its assault sling, he slipped his eight-inch Randall stiletto from its sheath. Firelight danced along the razor-sharp blade as he spun it so it lay against the inside of his forearm. His left arm was extended, fist closed, across his body in a protective block. Able to fully see his attacker, he noticed the tiny glimmer of a familiar gold emblem pinned onto the man's woolen cap.

Stennmaker hadn't wasted any time when he heard the Huey's door gunner begin to blast them out of their snug positions outside the rear entrance of the lab. Knowing from his military experience that the entire crew would be wearing night-vision devices, and that the gunner would be able to see them as easily as if it were high noon, he dropped to his belly and snaked his way back into the depths of the thicket where he'd positioned himself.

His goal had originally been to link up with one of their own choppers and order the pilot to fly him out of the killing zone that was Alpine. After the Huey's appearance it was pretty damned obvious that the government was the one whacking them, and Stennmaker had no immediate plans that included federal prison. He'd just reached the path leading to the rear gate when the trees began spitting bits of bark as reams of .223 fire poured into the wood line from angry SAWs.

Balling up behind a thick pine, he realized he'd somehow lost his pistol during his flight from the Huey. When the abrupt barrage of fire ended, he slipped onto the concrete trail and sprinted toward the gate, his hand gripping the UDT knife he wore under his sweater.

He had just heard the Bells overhead and had accepted that his chances of freedom were now lessened by two when the ferocious blast of the lab once again drove him into the ground. Fearing that the helipad was now unsafe, he angled toward the southwest corner of the compound, loping through the trees. If he could get clear of the lodge he would work his way into the surrounding hills and then sit tight. He knew the highway was close, and that meant there was always the chance of separating a car from its owner.

That was when he spotted the tail gunner for the team that had hit them, clearly visible in the light of the brightly burning inferno behind them. Rage flushed through Stennmaker. Watching the other two break into the thick bushes that ran the length of the culvert, Stennmaker broke from his own cover and hit the man squarely in the back as he turned to cross over himself. Planning to drag Thornton down into the ice-filled ditch and snap his neck, he was surprised to find himself staring into the single eye of a CAR-15. When the raider shoved the carbine behind him and drew a wicked-looking dagger from his pistol belt, Stennmaker knew the gun was either unloaded or that the man was crazy. *Nobody* fought with knives anymore. Sucking in a deep breath of cordite-tainted air, he pulled his own 7 1/4-inch blade from its scabbard and lowered himself into the on-guard position they'd taught him at Little Creek.

Warily the two men eyed each other. Forced to fight within the narrow confines of the shallow moat, each waited for the other to make his opening move. Stennmaker suddenly scooted forward, feinting toward the man's belly, then slashing quickly upward into the throat. Taking a half-step back, the other man twisted away from Stennmaker's thrust, then whipped his blade forward and across as Stennmaker's arm was left unprotected. The stiletto's blade bit into the sweater Stennmaker wore, slicing into his forearm.

As he completed the cut, the other man stepped back with his left foot, the move putting distance between himself and his adversary. As he did so he spun the perfectly balanced fighting knife in his hand, pulling it to hip level with the blade's tip pointing forward.

Stennmaker gasped at the jolt of pain that streaked up his arm when the man's knife connected. Keeping his eyes on the man in front of him, the stocky merc pulled his own blade back, grabbing a handful of snow from the crusted bank. Both men were oblivious to the sounds from the lodge several hundred feet away, their full attention on each other as the seconds seemed to stretch into minutes.

With a yell, Stennmaker threw the glob of compressed ice crystals directly into the other's face. At the same time he leaped forward, his blade moving at incredible speed as he transferred the power from his twisting hips and torso into his arm. His face creased itself into a twisted mask of sadistic victory as he watched the man instinctively flinch at the snowy diversion. But as he reached the spot where his opponent had stood he was greeted with a phantom's embrace.

Thornton was already moving in for the kill as he saw the rogue SEAL grab a handful of snow. As the man bounded forward, a cloud of ice crystals exploding from his hand, Bo dropped to a kneeling position and grabbed the knife-wielding thug's arm just behind the elbow as it passed harmlessly over his head. Digging his fingers and thumb into the major nerve center located there, he heard his victim cry out as intense pressure broke Stennmaker's hold on his knife. Hearing the rare weapon fall from his opponent's numbed hand, Thornton drove his Randall up between the man's legs. Stennmaker's head rolled back, an unearthly howl erupted from his lips as eight full inches of steel slammed through his scrotum and into the deepest region of his guts. Pushing upward onto his toes in a vain attempt to dislodge himself the hired gun's knees buckled as Thornton twisted the blade sideways, ripping it downward and out.

Releasing the mortally wounded man's arm, Thornton grabbed a handful of his sweater and proceeded to jackhammer the dripping blade into the man's lower abdomen until he felt the body go limp against him.

Rising quickly, Thornton stepped back, allowing the bloodied mass to fall face forward at his feet. Not bothering to wipe his blade clean, Thornton shoved the Randall into its sheath and climbed out of the open-ended grave where Stennmaker lay. Less than five minutes had passed since the team shot its way out of Alpine's cellar. Thornton figured that Silver must have taken Lee directly to the LZ.

Climbing out of the culvert, he stopped and turned toward the lodge. Nearly three-quarters of it was engulfed in flames, and a knot of men stood at the far end of the outdoor deck. Obviously they were fighting with each other, attempting to scramble down the single stairway.

Behind them, intense heat was fanned by a gentle breeze coming from the northeast, tongues of greedy fire licking their way out through the shattered sliding glass door and onto the deck. Thornton also smelled the all-too-familiar odor of cooking flesh, Dancer's Christmas playground now an unholy crematorium.

Turning away from the nightmare, he came face to face with what he swore was a specter from Hell's greatest depths. The Monk growled with glee as he swung his huge fist at the shocked One-Zero's head, knocking Thornton into the ditch he'd just climbed out of. Shaking his head, Bo struggled to regain his senses, rolling away just as the biker's heavy leather boots slammed into the ground where he'd fallen.

Thornton scrabbled his way over Stennmaker's rapidly cooling corpse. His combat instincts once again functioning, he now sought to escape the high-stepping boots of the scorched vision before him. The huge creature smashed his way through the dead SEAL's remains, stopping to deliver several steel-toed kicks to the cadaver's temple before turning his attentions once again toward Thornton.

Reaching underneath his combat tunic, Bo jerked the heavy Russian springblade from its holster. Swiftly pulling the metal sheath away from the seven-inch Crain blade, he released the weapon's safety and aimed it at the advancing biker.

The Monk stopped. As his brain registered what the commando held, he began laughing, the din an evil rumble that came from deep within his feral soul. Without warning, he leaped toward his opponent, fingers outstretched and greedy as they sought to wrap themselves around his throat.

Adjusting his aim at the form now flying toward him, Thornton pressed the ballistic knife's trigger and felt his blade fly free. Rolling rapidly to his left, he managed to evade the giant's body as it plowed, with a grunt, into the snow beside him. Clawing for his Browning, Thornton turned to see the biker raise himself on his hands and knees, the blade's stabilizer protruding from where it had punctured his larynx.

Snarling, Thornton released the locked and loaded 9mm from its holster and thumbed back the hammer. He had gone into a total killing rage, his warrior's control gone as the scent and fear of his own possible extinction overcame him. Pushing the barrel against the dull-witted biker's skull he began pulling the trigger as quickly as he could. Round after round rocketed its way through the thick bone structure, spraying slippery chunks of brain matter over both men as Thornton's rage expended itself.

Finally the weapon's slide locked to the rear, its magazine empty.

Shaking like a leaf from massive injections of adrenaline now coursing through his veins, Thornton stood. As he rolled the apelike body over to retrieve the edged projectile still embedded in the biker's throat, he was overcome by the rancid smell of shit, piss, and blood. Staggering against the opposite wall he gagged, a thin trickle of bile and stomach fluids running down his chin as he fought to compose himself. Successful, he avoided looking directly into the pool of human stew at his feet while he reassembled the springblade and hooked it into its carrier.

Grabbing the Colt by its suppressor, he swung it forward and dropped the empty magazine. Slipping a fresh one into the well, he repeated the process with his Browning. Off in the distance he heard two successive detonations; what they were he couldn't be sure. Holding his position for an extra moment, he searched the brightly lit grounds for any further movement. Not seeing any, and anxious to rejoin the team, Thornton cleared the earthen wall with one leap and ran toward the clatter of an inbound chopper.

Silver dragged his wounded companion through the hole they'd cut in the fence, while the echoes of Thornton's Browning washed over them from back within the woods. Trusting that his friend could take care of himself, he helped his brother in arms to his feet. "Where's Bo?" grunted Lee.

"He's back in the bush pulling a rear guard for us. Let's get the hell to the LZ before Frank comes in . . . Bo'll be pissed if we miss our taxi."

Skimming over the treetops, Frank Hartung listened impatiently for his team to come up on the radio. After spreading a little Christmas cheer amongst Dancer's goons, he'd ordered the pilot to head for their extraction orbit three klicks west of the helipad. They'd just missed the first of the Bells as they entered their own racetrack. Hartung knew exactly what was being planned by Dancer as the first bird touched down on the burning building's roof. He told the pilot what to do, and they dropped into a tiny hole in the forest to watch as the second Bell flew past them. Rising out of the ground like a winged apparition, they spotted Dancer's bird as it crossed in front of them, heading toward the open plains. Hartung ordered pursuit as both Bells linked up and set a course for the nearby airport.

Skimming above the ground, Hartung checked his map and nodded in satisfaction. Less than a half mile away was an expanse of broken lava rock over which their direction of flight would take them. Slipping his hand into his flight suit, the grinning sergeant major removed the remote detonator Silver had left him and flicked its "fire" switch to the ready position. Hearing the pilot's verbal that their quarry had entered the killing field, Hartung pushed the tiny lever forward.

Holding on tightly as the Huey pulled a hard right, Hartung

was greeted by the sight of two separate balls of flame crashing into the volcanic rockpiles below them. "*Sin loi*, Mr. Dancer," he muttered. "What goes around comes around."

The Huey was just beginning its glide toward the LZ when the co-pilot spoke. "Hey, Frank, I got two people on the 'zone' at my one o'clock."

Hartung leaned out against his monkey strap, his feet firmly planted on the skid, gloved hand maintaining his balance as he held on to the forward position of the ship's doorframe. "Damn!" he cursed. "Looks like one of 'em is carrying the other, doesn't it?"

The crew chief scanned the opposite side of the LZ, relaying to Hartung that there were no personnel on his side of the ship. As the pilot began to settle in for a landing, the two ground-pounders jogged toward the chopper. "Stand by to receive personnel!" ordered Hartung once the skids touched the earth's snowy surface. Leaping out before they had firmly settled, Frank ran to meet the two men. Recognizing Silver, he grabbed Lee's other arm and swung it over his neck. Together they dragged the now-exhausted man to the door of the Huey, where the crew chief waited, Hartung's SAW in his hands.

"Where's Bo?" shouted the sergeant major.

"I don't know," replied Silver, his voice ragged from the night's exertions. "He was with us up until a few minutes ago, then I heard gunfire behind us. Lee is pretty fucked up so I just kept moving."

"Ya done right, Jay. If anyone's gonna get out of that snake pit, it'll be Thornton. Are you all right?"

Silver nodded. "Yeah. Just some cuts and bruises. I—"

Hartung cut the man off as he spotted a figure break from the tree line. Whoever it was, he was moving directly toward them at a steady pace. Pushing the Minimi's barrel down, Hartung cautioned the anxious crew chief. "Let's see who it is, Chief . . . although I can just about tell you now by the way the bastard runs."

Picking his way between trees and bushes, Thornton ran a zig-zag pattern without opposition until he reached the fence line. Hearing the steady cadence of the helicopter's turbine, he rapidly climbed the cyclone barrier, dropping feet first onto the other side. Knowing Silver would be moving toward the bird by now, he dropped to one knee and remained motionless, careful not to attract a protective burst of Minimi fire from Frank's gun as they touched down. Pulling his goggles back on, Thornton was relieved to see they hadn't been damaged by the night's fighting. Focusing on the chopper, he watched as his two teammates reached safety, then stood and began a methodical trot toward the Huey himself.

"Get on board," exclaimed Hartung as Thornton became recognizable. "As usual you're dirty, wet, and late!"

While the crew chief hurriedly secured them, Thornton yelled into his closest friend's ear. "How's Lee and Jay?"

Hartung patted his weary One-Zero on the leg as the chopper's rotor began to lift them off the ground, nose tilting slightly earthward as the ship picked up speed and altitude. "They're both okay . . . we were wondering what was keeping you."

Thornton changed the subject by asking about Dancer's helicopters.

"Me and the boys here dropped them a coupla miles out as they were heading for the airport. Billings's crew will be able to confirm who was on board once they've had a chance to sift through the wreckage," replied Hartung.

Scooting back into the safety of the Huey, Thornton snugged himself up against the ship's fire wall. The four of them exchanged glances in the dimly lit cabin, then closed their eyes as the pilot radioed ahead that they were inbound with wounded.

Behind them on the ground, Bailey and a swarm of DEA agents swept through the grounds that had been Alpine, its still-burning fires clearly revealing the destruction wreaked by Thornton's team.

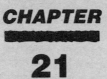
He stood on the beach watching as she carefully stepped from tide pool to tide pool, a chill wind blowing her hair so that she had to hold it in one hand. Overhead, gulls wheeled and screamed at each other in mock combat, every so often landing on the sand to peck for hidden tidbits. His hands were pushed deeply into the pockets of his Levi's, a leather flight jacket holding the cold at bay. Despite the sun being hidden by a heavy cloud bank, he still wore sunglasses. She was the only one he let get close to him as he sorted out the last few weeks.

The team had broken up two days before. Lee, of course, had been flown to a private hospital in California as soon as they had landed at the MSS. Silver, Hartung, and he had returned to the coast to square away the FOB and sit through several days of debriefings by Bailey and his people. Frank's flight had left within hours of Calvin's releasing them.

Jason Silver wired his sister to send whatever he had left behind, and found himself an apartment in the town of Seaside. Confessing that he had nothing to go back to except ugly women, Silver asked if Thornton would mind him being a neighbor of sorts. Bo welcomed the company. He had moved back into his condo at the Breacon. He thought about looking for some land. San Diego had lost its charm, compared to the wild freeness of the rugged Oregon coast.

The girl looked up from her explorations and waved to him. Slowly returning the greeting, he gingerly shrugged his battered and bruised shoulders. There was still a slight ringing in his head from where the biker had clobbered him, and splinters continued to push through his skin, the short-term results of being too close to things exploding.

Overall he felt pretty lucky.

"What are you looking so somber about?" asked Linda as she pushed herself against him.

Putting his arms around her and staring down into her lovely face, he decided she was right; he had nothing to be somber about. The DEA had found few survivors after the conflagration at Alpine, and the government had confiscated the property under the Rico Act. The affair was reported in the media as a rivalry between warring Los Angeles drug factions, the Monk's unexpected participation having given credence to the cover Billings had concocted.

More important, everyone got paid.

"It's chilly. Do you want to go in?" she whispered against his ear.

Gazing once more at the broad expanse of ocean, he nodded. Then, draping his arm over her shoulders and turning them both around, they began the short walk back up the beach.